Get her out ... **himself firm**

'She's all wrong ~~for you. But ...~~ Surely that should say something,' he muttered as he retraced his steps down the hallway to his study, wondering how his well-ordered life had altered so dramatically in such a short space of time.

A shout of laughter came from next door and he immediately knew the answer. Halley Ryan. She'd erupted into his life and turned it upside down. Five days she'd been here. Five full days of walking a tightrope—and the crazy thing was that the unbalanced sensation was starting to become familiar to him.

Lucy Clark began writing romance in her early teens and immediately knew she'd found her 'calling' in life. After working as a secretary in a busy teaching hospital, she turned her hand to writing medical romance. She currently lives in South Australia with her husband and two children. Lucy largely credits her writing success to the support of her husband, family and friends.

You can visit Lucy's website at www.lucyclark.net or email her at lucyclark@optusnet.com.au

Recent titles by the same author:

THE CONSULTANT'S CONFLICT
THE SURGEON'S SECRET
THE DOCTOR'S DILEMMA
THE FAMILY HE NEEDS

THE OUTBACK MATCH

BY
LUCY CLARK

To Aunty Rae—with much love
Ps 25:4-5

First published in Great Britain 2002
Harlequin Mills & Boon Limited,
Eton House, 18-24 Paradise Road, Richmond, Surrey TW9 1SR

© Lucy Clark 2002

ISBN 0 263 83073 X

Set in Times Roman 10½ on 12 pt.
03-0602-48524

Printed and bound in Spain
by Litografía Rosés, S.A., Barcelona

CHAPTER ONE

'YOU'RE late!'

Halley Ryan glanced up to where the deep, impatient tone had come from, and gazed into a pair of frowning blue eyes. She felt her heart skip a beat and returned her attention to the ground, where she continued to pick up the papers that had fallen from her grasp as she'd rushed towards the front entrance to Heartfield District Hospital.

Her new colleague was one good-looking man. Tall, too—just the way she liked them. Perhaps her two weeks here in outback Victoria might be fun after all. She'd thought it would be all work and no play. A smile twitched at her lips as she risked another glance at him. He was still scowling down at her but he was as gorgeous as she'd thought. Belatedly, she realised he was waiting for an explanation.

'Sorry,' she explained as she shoved the papers loosely back into the file. She stood to her full height of five feet, four inches and smiled at the man before her. 'Believe it or not, I got lost. You must be Dr Pearson.' She gazed up at him. He *was* tall—about six feet four, she guessed—but, then, most people were taller than her.

'I'd offer my hand but...' She shrugged, her smile still in place. 'It's a bit difficult at the moment.' Halley shifted her stance and the file she'd just gathered up moved precariously. She had her bag slung over her shoulder, her briefcase in one hand, her favourite medical text beneath her arm and in the other she held several other books and files.

'Hmm.' Dr Pearson raised one exasperated eyebrow, before turning on his heel and walking back into the hospital. Halley watched him go, her smile disappearing. What was *his* problem? She frowned as she followed him into the hospital, her eyes taking a while to focus from the bright morning light outside. She had expected an offer of help from him, even though she'd probably have refused it. Was chivalry really dead?

'Through here.' Dr Pearson's tone was brisk and Halley continued to follow him down a freshly painted hospital corridor to a section marked ADMINISTRATION. Now that her eyes had adjusted to the internal light, Halley watched with delight the way her new colleague walked. It was direct, with a purpose. The cut of his suit trousers did nothing to hide the curve of his butt. As for his crisp white shirt and no-nonsense tie, they were as stiff and starched as the man himself appeared to be. His arms swung in military fashion by his sides, and she had to stretch her own stride to keep up with his.

'This will be your office. Mine is two doors up. The room in between is the file room.' He glared down at the files in her hands. 'It is neat and orderly and that's the way I expect it to stay.'

'Yessir,' she teased, her voice like that of a soldier. Although the instant she'd done it, she realised it had probably been the wrong thing to do. Instinctively, she knew this man wasn't used to being teased! Well, perhaps she could change all that!

Dr Pearson's deep blue eyes flashed with annoyance but he didn't say anything more. A brisk nod in her direction and he was gone, leaving her standing at the door of her new office.

'Whew!' Halley unburdened herself, dumping everything on top of the neat, organised desk before slumping down into her chair. It creaked as she leaned back and placed her feet up on the desk. It would do. Not the most comfortable chair in the world, but for the two weeks that she'd be here she'd get by.

She took a deep breath and thought about Dr Max Pearson, her new colleague. He was quite handsome with his short dark brown hair and gorgeous blue eyes, even though they had been rather icy. Halley wondered what it would be like to gaze into those eyes once they'd thawed a little, or if a smile ever touched them. Oh, yes, there was definitely something bothering him and she had a sneaking suspicion it had to do with the first two words he'd said to her.

'You're late.' Halley said them out loud, mimicking his deep voice as best she could. She shook her head and grimaced wryly. 'Two weeks, Ryan,' she told herself. 'You're only here for two weeks so no more jokes, keep quiet and do your job.'

'Sounds like good advice to me,' a deep, resonant voice said from the doorway, startling Halley so much that she overbalanced and fell backwards in her chair.

Thankful that she'd worn her usual trousers, Halley quickly scrambled her way out, picked up the chair and smiled at her colleague as though this were an everyday occurrence.

'Clinic starts in precisely two minutes so we'd better go.' Max Pearson took a step away from the doorway and waited for her to move. Again he led the way, walking in front of her as though he might catch some awful germ.

'It looks as though the hospital has been recently painted,' she said conversationally, hoping he'd slow his pace and perhaps walk beside her.

'Very observant,' he replied over his shoulder.

'Have you worked here long?' she tried again.

'Ten years.'

'Oh.' Halley frowned. From what the Victorian Department for Health had said, the Heartfield District Hospital had been manned by a six-monthly rotation of general practitioners. They hadn't said anything about having a permanent GP within the community. Then again, perhaps Dr Pearson didn't live within the community. Perhaps he rotated through a few different outback districts and just happened to be at Heartfield District today. There was only one way to find out.

'Do you live around here?'

'Yes.'

Halley nodded understandingly. No wonder he was so cold towards her. After all, she was here to evaluate the hospital and possibly recommend it for closure.

They walked into a room that was filled with patients. A chorus of, 'Mornin', Doc,' came from a few people as they either smiled or waved to him. He briefly introduced her to the receptionist and a few of the nursing staff.

'This is Sheena Albright. She's the ''matron'' of the hospital. Theatre sister, ward sister—you name it, she does it. If you have any queries, she's the person to speak to.'

'Welcome,' Sheena offered.

'Who's the lucky new doc?' one woman asked, and Dr Pearson turned to look at his patients.

'A very good question, Mrs Smythe. This is Dr Ryan. She's here for the next two weeks to help out with clinics, house calls and medical procedures.'

'Oh,' said Mrs Smythe. 'So *she's* the one who's gonna decide whether the hospital should close.'

'What? She's the judge and jury?' a man asked.

'All right, settle down,' Max Pearson said. 'We've already discussed this topic. This isn't the town meeting. This is a hospital clinic and it's past time we started. Don't you agree, Dr Ryan?' He looked at Halley, as did every other pair of eyes in the room.

'Ah…yes. Good idea.' She turned and entered one of the consulting rooms, closing the door behind her. She leaned against the wall and closed her eyes. How was she supposed to work effectively when she had all *that* to deal with? Halley realised that she was a bit flustered and forced herself to do some deep breathing exercises.

When her pulse rate was back to normal, she quickly checked the drawers, familiarising herself with the layout and supplies in the cupboards. Taking one last deep breath, she closed her eyes and gave her arms and shoulders a shake before crossing to the door, a bright smile fixed firmly in place. She walked out to the waiting area where a hush quickly fell over the room and she instinctively knew they'd all been discussing her.

She turned to the receptionist. 'Case-notes, please?' The receptionist pointed to a pile and Halley took the top one. 'Mrs Smythe?'

There was no answer, but everyone turned to look at the lady who had spoken before. She was slowly edging forward in her chair, gripping the handlebars of a metal walking frame. Halley immediately crossed to her side to help.

'Thank ya,' Mrs Smythe grumbled. 'Ya've got manners,' she said with a nod. 'That's a start.'

Everyone in the room watched them slowly progress towards the consulting room and she realised it was no fluke that Mrs Smythe had been called as her first patient. She escorted the elderly woman in, curious as to her role in the community. She didn't have long to wait.

'I've lived in Heartfield all me life,' Mrs Smythe said as soon as the consulting-room door was closed. 'Oh, sure, I've travelled, but this is where me home is and I've known most of the people out there…' she waggled a gnarled, arthritic finger at the door '…since before they was born.'

Halley could tell that the community probably depended a lot on Mrs Smythe's opinion. 'Would it be easier for you to get up onto the examination couch first, rather than sitting down and then having to get up again? That way I can check the range of motion in your joints more easily.'

'I'm not here for a check-up,' Mrs Smythe told her briskly as she continued over to the chair. Halley helped her to sit down.

'Oh?' She flicked open the file and noted that the other woman had been reviewed by Dr Pearson only the previous week. 'Well, then…' Halley settled back in her own chair. 'What can I do for you?'

'I want to know ya views on closing our hospital, because I'll tell you right now that the community is prepared to stand behind young Maxwell and will support him in the fight to keep it open.'

Halley had to control the urge not to smile at Mrs Smythe's reference to 'young Maxwell'. He was certainly young but the title made him seem inconsequential—which the man was definitely not.

'Fair enough. First of all, I'd like to say that I was chosen for this job; I didn't apply for it. I've just returned from working overseas for a few years and was approached by the Victorian Department for Health to evaluate this hospital.'

'Oh, so ya only here to evaluate, then, are ya?'

'Mrs Smythe, in my defence, I'm not the sole judge and jury, as was suggested. Once I've completed my evaluation, I'll be giving a recommendation as to how the VDH should proceed. I should warn you that they can still overrule that recommendation after a board has reviewed all—'

'Oh, stuff and nonsense!' Mrs Smythe interrupted.

'Those department people have already made up their minds to close this hospital and sending ya here is obviously just a formality.' Mrs Smythe had heard enough as she started to wriggle out of her chair. Halley quickly came around to help her up. 'I suppose ya've done this kind of thing before? Closed other hospitals down?'

'Actually, Mrs Smythe, of the three hospitals that I've evaluated, two have remained open.'

'And the third one?'

'I recommended that it close.'

'I see.'

'No, you don't. The hospital in question was decrepit and falling down—beyond repair. A new hospital had been built in the neighbouring district and the residents would have to travel a further ten minutes to reach it. The circumstances were completely different from those here in Heartfield.' Mrs Smythe was heading towards the door and Halley felt compelled to change the other woman's opinion of her.

'Look. I know the community here sees me as the harbinger of doom but I'm only here to do a job. If you disagree with me about the job that's one thing, but for people to hold that against *me*, the *person*, is unfair and unjust. In doing so, they're the ones acting as judge and jury and not giving me a fair go at all.'

Mrs Smythe stopped shuffling and smiled at Halley. 'That's what I wanted to hear. Good girl. If ya fight like that for yaself, then I know ya'll put up a good fight to save our hospital.'

After Mrs Smythe had left, Halley was amazed to find her hands shaking. What had she gotten herself into by accepting this job? She was used to a bit of hostility when she came into a town with the prospect of evaluating a hospital, but these people seemed to genuinely dislike her sight unseen!

Halley called upon her professional attitude and that helped her to wade through the rest of the clinic, enduring the curious and sometimes resentful glances she received from various patients.

'How'd it go?'

Halley didn't need to look at her doorway to see who was talking. She'd only met Max Pearson a few hours ago, and hadn't really had that much contact with him during those hours, but still she'd recognise that voice anywhere.

'Not bad.' Halley stood, making sure the desk was as tidy as when she'd first entered the room. 'What's next on the agenda, Dr Pearson?'

'Make it Max.' He shrugged nonchalantly. 'House calls.' With that, he walked away. Halley shook her head and quickly followed him, saying a quick thank you and good-bye to the receptionist and nursing staff. She didn't want to get lost in the hospital. That would be humiliating and she'd had just about enough humiliation for one day—and it wasn't even over yet!

She glanced at her watch as Max headed back towards Administration. One o'clock—no wonder she was starving. She hadn't thought as far ahead as lunch when she'd risen at the crack of dawn this morning to drive the three hours from Melbourne to Heartfield. Breakfast, yes, but lunch—that had been a long way off.

Max appeared a moment later, carrying a black medical bag in one hand and a briefcase in the other. 'Let's go.' He walked past her and out to the main entrance.

'Please, let him say we're stopping for lunch first,' she mumbled softly to herself, but didn't dare voice the suggestion. She wasn't *that* hungry. No doubt Max would have healthy sandwiches in his briefcase. He seemed the type of person who would only eat healthy food. Perhaps there was a woman in his life who made his lunch every morning.

Woman? Where had that come from? Halley frowned. Up until now, she'd thought of him as a bachelor. He stopped beside a four-wheel-drive and placed his bags carefully in the back. Halley watched him closely, her gaze immediately travelling to his left hand to check for a wedding ring. The plain gold band was noticeably absent and she breathed a sigh of relief.

Her frown deepened at her reaction. Then again, perhaps he was married but simply chose not to wear a band. A lot of men did. There was only one way to find out—she'd have to ask him.

'Well, don't just stand there, Halley. In you get,' he ordered, and she realised she'd been staring. She turned away and headed for the passenger door, feeling embarrassed once more. What must he think of her? She climbed in and did up her seat belt.

'I have no idea how you could have got lost this morning,' Max said as he turned the car onto the road. 'There's only one road in and out of this town.'

'First of all,' she said, her voice calm, 'there is one *main* road in and out of this town but quite *a few* other roads leading in all sorts of directions.'

'I faxed clear and concise directions to the Victorian Department for Health over a week ago.'

'Well, I've got news for you, Max, I don't work for the VDH.'

He looked at her then, a deep frown creasing his forehead. 'They said they were sending someone from their department to evaluate the hospital.' He returned his attention to the road, waving now and then to people as they drove by.

She shifted in her seat so she was facing him more. 'I'm

a medical professional, Max, sent here as a contractor to do the job of evaluating this hospital. It has nothing to do with me as a person.'

Max didn't reply to this. Instead he flicked on his indicator and left the dirt road they'd been following, turning onto a track barely wide enough to take the car.

Around a corner, up a small mound, on and on the track seemed to go, and Max stayed silent as he navigated the undulating terrain. He went over a big bump and Halley hit her head on the window before bouncing back to the headrest.

'Ow,' she said, and rubbed the injured spot.

'Sorry. I've already spoken to Dan about fixing his driveway but he says it helps keep people away.'

Driveway? This track was someone's excuse for a driveway? 'Dan sounds like a barrel of laughs,' Halley mumbled as they came around one last corner to see an old farmhouse standing before them. Three large blue heelers headed directly for them at top speed, their barks carrying loudly and excitedly through the air.

Max pulled up right outside the front door, cut the engine and undid his seat belt. 'Let me have a look,' he said, and reached out his hands towards her head.

Halley shrank back for a second. 'Oh, I'm sure it's just a bump. I'll be fine.'

'If you'll just let me have a quick look,' he stated again in that no-nonsense voice that brooked no argument. He undid her seat belt and beckoned for her to come closer.

Halley shifted in her seat and leaned towards him, tilting her head. One warm hand came up to cup her chin, angling her head so he could see, the other was placed gently on the top of her scalp, holding it firmly. The dogs outside were still barking and jumping around the car, but their noise and presence faded as Halley became increasingly conscious of Max's hands on her face. The warmth of his skin touching hers sent shock waves through her system and Halley's eyes widened at the reaction.

She focused her gaze straight ahead, but as that meant she was looking directly at Max's shirt she wasn't sure whether it was a good idea. The pull of the fabric emphasised his firm upper arm muscles. Halley breathed in deeply, his aftershave assaulting her senses. Her heart started to pound an increased rhythm and her mouth became dry.

He moved his hand from beneath her chin to tenderly run his fingers over the lump that was obviously starting to form. Halley winced slightly.

'Sorry. Just a bump,' he said as he pulled away and cleared his throat. 'You'll do fine.' With that, he opened the door, ordered the dogs to sit, which they obediently did and climbed from the car.

Halley couldn't move. For a whole three seconds she merely stared at him as he walked around the car to retrieve his medical bag. She closed her eyes momentarily, willing her breathing to return to normal.

You're only here for two weeks, Halley told herself as she reached for the doorhandle. And, besides, you don't even *know* the man. She shook her head, searching for a rational explanation for her reaction to Max's touch, but realised she'd have to do it later as he was standing by the front door, shrugging into his jacket, glaring at her with impatience.

'Sorry,' she mumbled as she climbed from the car. The dogs barked louder at this stranger who had dared to set foot on their property. Halley held out her hand so they could sniff her but she was unable to move her feet as they crowded around her.

'Sit!' Max issued the command again, the dogs immediately leaving her alone and doing as they were told. She wondered for a moment at the animals' reaction to this man. It was as though he were their master. Perhaps he called here so often they were used to him.

Halley walked past the obedient dogs, whose tails were still twitching, and followed Max into the house. She noted that he didn't knock or ring a bell and that the door was unlocked—although people in the country rarely locked their doors, she rationalised.

'Hello,' he called loudly upon entering.

'Be right there, Max,' a male voice called.

As they stood there, waiting, Halley's stomach growled. Max slowly turned and glared down his nose at her.

'What?' She shrugged her shoulders. 'I can't control it.'

'You might want to try putting food into it,' he said quietly.

'Be glad to. When's lunchtime?' she whispered back urgently.

He didn't answer as they both heard footsteps heading their way. 'Max.' The man who entered the room nodded and held out his hand. Halley watched the two men shake hands.

'Dan.'

Dan was a few inches shorter than Max, probably about six feet one, she guessed. He had grey hair and hazel eyes. His nose was crooked, indicating a break in earlier years. He was dressed in charcoal-grey suit trousers, a striped blue shirt and a tie with an insignia on it. He was slightly overweight and Halley decided he probably ate too many corporate lunches. He looked very out of place in the down-to-earth country homestead which was cluttered with books and photographs.

'How is she today?' Max asked.

'Better. Kylie was around earlier today to put a new

dressing on. I wasn't here at the time but Mum said Kylie was happy with the progress.'

'Good.'

'And who do we have here?' Dan asked as he turned to look at Halley. His eyes skimmed her neat and professional attire, but when his gaze met hers she was shocked to see dislike in the stranger's eyes.

'This is Dr Ryan.'

'Oh, for crying out loud—she's a *woman*!' Dan pointed to her and then shook his head. 'We've no hope, then. The hospital will definitely close.'

CHAPTER TWO

HALLEY bristled at Dan's words. What did her sex have to do with anything? 'Is there a problem?' she asked, not accustomed to being passed over like that when she was meeting a new acquaintance. When Dan didn't reply, she turned to Max.

He held up his hand, stopping her from saying anything else. 'As I've been saying all along, Dan, it's customary for the Victorian Department for Health to send someone to evaluate country hospitals from time to time. The fact that this evaluation may result in the closure of the hospital is yet to be decided.'

'Yes, yes, so you said last week at the town meeting, but the fact remains, Max, that whatever she says goes.'

'That's not quite—' Halley began, but again Max held up his hand for silence and glared at her.

'Dr Ryan's credentials are impressive to say the least, Dan, and you know how much trouble we've had trying to secure a second permanent GP here. Having doctors coming and going every six months just so they can get their provider numbers from saying they've done their time in the country is starting to get on my nerves.'

'Well, if she has her way, then you'll definitely be all on your own *and* with no hospital to work from.'

'I prefer to reserve judgement until I've read Dr Ryan's evaluation. This district needs a hospital—'

'Agreed,' Dan said, but Max continued.

'But your methods of making Dr Ryan out to be the enemy are only making matters worse.'

Halley felt as though she were watching a tennis match, looking from one man to the other as they stood there, discussing her. The only bright spot in this ludicrous situation was knowing that Max was being open-minded about the situation. It was some consolation, but Dan's treatment made her body go rigid with anger and he wasn't even giving her the opportunity to defend herself.

'You were wrong to call that town meeting last week, and you're wrong to be so rude to her now,' Max declared, his voice still calm and controlled.

'I am the shire president,' Dan declared as he thrust his chest out, preening like a peacock. '*And* your prospective father-in-law.'

Halley looked at Max. Prospective *father-in-law*? He was engaged? Max was engaged? Why did she suddenly feel a constriction in her heart? She lifted her chin slightly. So? He was engaged. Big deal. Good luck to him and, boy, was he going to need it with Dan as his future father-in-law. She sincerely hoped Dan's daughter had a much better temper than her old man!

'I not only demand respect but I deserve it. I've given you permission to marry Christina and if you're going to be in my family then I expect you to follow the rules.'

Halley continued to watch Max. He appeared unperturbed by Dan's outrage, as though he'd heard it all before.

'This has nothing to do with your family, Dan. It has to do with my job as Director of Heartfield District Hospital. A position, I might add, that reports to the hospital board and not to the shire president. Now, if you'll excuse me, I didn't come here to discuss this with you. I came to see Clarabelle. If Dr Ryan and I don't get on with our house calls, we'll be running late for the rest of the day.'

With that, Max stepped around Dan, indicated that Halley should follow him and proceeded up a corridor.

He didn't apologise. He didn't say anything, and Halley wondered whether he was too preoccupied with his thoughts. However, when he knocked on a door and entered a bedroom, he was all ease and friendliness, the professional doctor with a caring bedside manner.

'I heard Dan blustering,' a woman, obviously Clarabelle, said as they crossed over to the large bed where she lay on top of the covers.

Max merely shrugged. Moments later, they all heard a car door slam and then the engine rev before the roar of the engine faded into the distance, leaving the homestead in peace again.

'Oh, and this must be the new doctor.' Clarabelle smiled brightly and held out her hand to Halley. 'No wonder Dan was in a state. A *female* doctor.' She giggled and Halley smiled. 'As far as my son is concerned, women are pretty objects to be adorned. Heaven forbid that we might actually have brains *and* choose to use them.'

Halley shook the woman's hand, guessing her to be in her mid-eighties. She had snow-white hair, bound in one long plait resting over her shoulder, and the bluest eyes Halley had ever seen.

'I'm pleased to meet you, Mrs…'

'Oh, call me Clarabelle. It makes me feel younger. What's your name, dear?'

'Halley. Halley Ryan.'

'Now, that's a pretty name.'

'Thank you. My parents have a love of astronomy and I was named after the great astronomer Edmund Halley, who discovered—'

'Halley's comet,' Clarabelle finished for her. 'How delightful.'

'Are you two going to gas-bag all day long?' Max asked as he took out his stethoscope. Even though his words were said in his usual calm tone, Halley noticed his eyes twinkling with delight, as though he was actually teasing.

'And what if we are?' Clarabelle asked. 'In fact, why don't you leave Halley here and go and do whatever else you have to do? I can tell immediately that she's a kindred spirit.'

'Sorry. No can do. Your dear Halley hasn't had any lunch yet, so the first stop after here is to fill that stomach of hers before introducing her to the rest of the patients on my house-call list.' Max sat down and listened to Clarabelle's chest, effectively silencing them all.

Halley noticed the large bandage on Clarabelle's leg, raising the immediate suspicion of a varicose ulcer. Max continued with the check-up but didn't remove the bandage as it still looked fine.

'Did Kylie leave any notes for me?' he asked, and Clarabelle nodded.

'Kylie's our district nurse,' Clarabelle informed Halley. 'Just in case Max hasn't told you about her. He's the strong, silent type. Doesn't like to talk too much,' she said in a mock whisper, and Halley chuckled, glancing at her colleague.

'So I've noticed.'

'Notes?' Max asked again and shook his head in mock disgust. 'Anyone would think you two had been lifelong friends the way you're giggling and nattering together.'

'As I said, kindred spirits.' Clarabelle spread her arms out wide as though there was nothing more to it. She pointed to the dressing-table by the door. 'Kylie left the notes there. Now, dear, I suppose he also hasn't mentioned the big Christmas dinner fundraiser the local church is holding this Saturday night?'

'No.' Halley shook her head.

'Men,' Clarabelle said with resignation. 'Anyway, it's a

special Christmas dinner this Saturday night. They do it every year—you know, Christmas in winter.'

'I've heard of them but never been.'

'It's great fun, isn't it, Max?'

'Just peachy,' he said dryly, not looking up from his perusal of the notes Kylie had left. Halley's smile increased at his blasé attitude.

'Oh, nonsense. The whole community is going to be there,' Clarabelle continued, and Halley decided right then that she probably wouldn't go. It seemed this community was holding her responsible for the fate of their hospital! 'There's a Christmas tree and a five-dollar lucky dip for little presents. All the relevant decorations, right up to the artificial mistletoe. And then there's the food! My word, it's delicious. Roast turkey with cranberry sauce, Christmas pudding with brandy cream for dessert, and everything in between.'

Halley's stomach rumbled and Clarabelle laughed. 'It appears you've sold my stomach on the idea,' she confessed. Max held out the notes to her and Halley quickly scanned them, her suspicion confirmed. They stated that Clarabelle's right varicose leg ulcer had improved within the last twenty-four hours and that treatment was working well. Kylie had cleaned and sterilised the area as well, noting that she would return tomorrow to do the same. Halley wanted to see the wound for herself and wondered whether she and Kylie might visit Clarabelle together the next day.

'Good. I'll give you your injection now to continue the treatment and one of us will see you tomorrow.' Max said.

'Oh, let it be Halley, *please*?' Clarabelle pleaded, and winked at Halley. Max didn't say anything until he'd given the injection and even then it was a noncommittal shrug.

'You be good,' he told his patient with a teasing smile.

'I will,' she promised. 'See you tomorrow, Halley. Bye,

Max.' Clarabelle waved to them both as they left her room. Halley waved back.

They were silent as they walked out to the car, the dogs barking wildly again. Halley stopped and waited for them to sniff her before giving them each a good stroke. 'Ooh, you look as though you're spoiled rotten by your mistress,' she crooned, before she heard Max clear his throat. She sighed and turned to look at him as he put his bag into the back of the vehicle. He was staring at her and shaking his head.

'Something wrong?' she asked as he shut the tailgate.

'Nothing.' Again he just stared.

'Max!'

'You really like those dogs, don't you?' he commented as the three blue heelers jumped and fussed around her. Halley giggled, trying to fight them off.

'What's not to like?' She laughed as one started to lick her hand. 'They're just big sooks.' She looked at the dogs in question. 'The lot of you. Yes, you're big, gorgeous sooks.'

'Hmm.' Max watched her for another second before ordering the dogs to sit. They did so immediately but turned accusing eyes to him for spoiling their fun. 'Clarabelle has an old outside laundry, just around the corner. Wash your hands and I'll take you to the café for lunch.'

She went in the direction he was pointing, calling over her shoulder, 'I had the impression you'd already eaten.' She quickly washed her hands and returned to find him sitting in the car, seat belt on, engine running. 'I thought you'd already eaten,' she said once more, feeling more relaxed in his company.

'I could do with a cup of coffee and a doughnut,' he told her with a nonchalant shrug.

Halley waved to the dogs as they sat wagging their tails.

She took a deep breath, feeling quite content and happy—
for the moment. Who knew what the community of
Heartfield would throw at her next? But at least she had an
ally.

At the end of Clarabelle's bumpy driveway Max turned
back towards town and soon they'd stopped outside a bakery coffee shop. There was a large poster in the window
and as Halley climbed from the car she saw a picture of a
Christmas tree and realised it was advertising the dinner
Clarabelle had mentioned.

She breathed in. The delightful aromas coming from the
shop were mouthwatering. She walked inside, gazing up at
the menu board with its large variety displayed before her.

'Made up your mind yet?' Max said quietly from behind
her. His mouth was very close to her ear, and as she turned
to look at him her shoulder brushed his arm.

'Sor—' The word stuck in her suddenly dry throat and
Halley quickly cleared it. 'Sorry,' she whispered. The
crowded coffee shop and the people around them seemed
to blur as Halley gazed into Max's blue eyes. They were
softer, more friendly than they'd been earlier that morning,
and she wasn't quite sure what had provoked the change.
She frowned slightly and forced herself to turn back to the
board.

'So what would you like?' Max asked as he stepped towards the counter. 'My treat.'

'Oh, no. I couldn't possibly accept,' Halley said, shaking
her head.

'Really? Well, unless you carry money around in your
pockets, which I'm almost positive you don't, you'll have
to accept.'

The mortification of her situation hit with full impact.
She had no money with her! How could she have been so
careless?

'As I said, Halley…' His tone was a bit softer as he read her expression. 'My treat.'

Halley looked at him for a moment before nodding. 'So long as you allow me to return the favour.'

'Deal.'

'Hello, Max,' a woman in her late sixties greeted him from behind the counter. 'The usual?'

'No thank you, Alice. Just coffee and doughnuts,' he said giving Alice his gorgeous smile. Halley watched the way he charmed the other woman just as he'd done Clarabelle—and she'd thought it had been his bedside manner! No. This man was a professional woman-charmer with a capital C.

'It's always the quiet ones you have to watch,' she murmured to herself.

'Pardon?' He turned to look at her.

'Nothing, just mumbling. Hi, I'm Halley Ryan.' She extended her hand to Alice. 'The new doctor here to evaluate the hospital.' In for a penny…she thought.

'Welcome,' Alice said, shaking her hand and smiling. 'Now, as this is the first time you'll be tasting our wares, I'd recommend the shepherd's pie. Cooked the traditional way, of course.'

'Of course,' Halley agreed, relieved she wasn't going to be snubbed by Alice. She placed her order and shook her head with embarrassment when Max paid for her meal. 'How about tomorrow?' she asked as they chose a table near the window.

'For?'

'Lunch. Let me buy you lunch tomorrow.'

He paused before saying, 'I'll check my diary and let you know.'

Diary? That was something Halley had managed to avoid—being a slave to a little book. She had a clear and concise way of filing her appointments and that was in her head. A mental diary, and she knew right at this moment that she was free for lunch tomorrow.

Max was an intriguing man, and so far she'd seen several facets of his personality. She wanted to see deep down into his soul and share the things he'd never shared with anyone. The thought startled her and she shifted uncomfortably in her chair. What was she *thinking*? This man was her colleague. She'd do well to remember that. Not to mention the fact that he was also an engaged man!

'Max, I'd like to thank you.'

'For what?' He lounged back in his seat, stretching his long legs out to the side.

'For not prejudging me.'

He smiled and his blue eyes twinkled with suppressed mirth. It took her breath away and Halley was glad to be sitting down.

'So you did have a hard time this morning.'

Halley returned his smile. 'Only with some patients. I think it's admirable that you're being fair about this evaluation. You could rant and rave like some other members in this community but you're not and…well…' She shrugged. 'I just wanted to say thanks.'

He glanced down at his shoes and Halley held her breath, waiting for him to speak.

'Here you go, Docs,' Alice said as she brought over their food, placing it in front of them. 'Enjoy,' she said, and left them alone again.

'You have no need to thank me,' he told her over the top of his cup. 'You're just doing your job. I understand that. Now eat. I don't think I can bear to hear your stomach growling any more.'

Halley laughed and nodded. 'Good idea.' She tucked into the food, eating with the hearty appetite she'd always had.

Max told her something of the patients they were due to

see. 'And our last call for today is an avid rock-climber who sustained a fall. He broke his leg in three places and sustained a minor concussion.'

'I know what that's like,' Halley said as she swallowed her mouthful.

'What—breaking your leg and having concussion?'

'The breaking of the leg part, yes, but I didn't have concussion. Didn't he have a helmet on?'

Max seemed surprised. 'Ah, yes. Yes, he did, but it had a bad crack in it. He's lucky to have escaped with just mild concussion and a fractured leg.'

Halley nodded knowingly. 'I climb. Is there a local group that meets regularly?'

Max's eyebrows almost hit his hairline as he regarded her closely. '*You* rock-climb?'

'Uh-huh,' she said as she forked in the last mouthful.

'But you're so...'

Halley smiled at him as she chewed, waiting for him to finish his sentence. He didn't. Instead, he finished his coffee.

'Chicken,' she teased. 'I believe the politically correct term you're searching for is vertically challenged. I may not be tall but that doesn't stop me from enjoying rock-climbing.'

'Have you been doing it long?'

'Before I could walk. When I was a toddler, my brothers used to make me climb up and get things Mum had put out of their reach. That way, if they were found out, they could say that innocent little Halley got it down. Of course I was never punished. I was too adorable for that.'

Max smiled. 'We'd better make a move or we'll be way behind schedule.'

'Thank you again for lunch,' Halley told him after they'd

said goodbye to Alice and the other staff before heading
out to the four-wheel-drive.

'It's been…educational. I don't think I've ever seen a
woman enjoy food the way you do.'

Halley frowned slightly. What was that supposed to
mean?

'Usually they order a salad and then pick away at it.
Now, I know women like to watch their weight, but surely
there's merit in eating a balanced diet rather than solely
rabbit food.'

'Agreed,' Halley said as he pulled out onto the road. 'I
guess because I race around for most of the day—'

'As well as rock-climbing,' he added with a grin.

'*And* rock-climbing, that I haven't really had to watch
my weight too much.'

'So tell me more about your brothers. How many do you
have?'

'Two. Jupiter and Mars. They're twins.'

'I beg your pardon?'

Halley smiled at her common slip. 'Sorry—that's their
nicknames. Jon is…' she tilted her head and looked at him
'…probably a bit taller than you and Marty, who's about
your height, has bright red hair. The nicknames fit, and as
I'm named after a comet…' She shrugged. 'My parents are
into astronomy,' she added.

'So you've said. What work does your father do?'

Halley was a little surprised at how chatty Max was being but supplied the information anyway. 'He's retired. So
is my mother. My brothers run the family business which—
before you ask—is Planet Electronics.'

Max glanced over at her and then back to the road.
'Planet Electronics? *That's* your family's business?'

'Yes.'

'Halley, that's a multi-million-dollar business.'

'So is telecommunications. So what?'

He nodded. 'Good point.'

So often—too many times for her to count—when people found out about Planet Electronics, they couldn't understand why she'd chosen medicine as a career. Well, the truth was, she wasn't the least bit interested in electronics and loved medicine.

'So how about you? Do you have any siblings?'

Max stared at the road ahead, slipping into silent mode once more.

'Now, that's not fair, Max,' she said after a minute's silence. 'I shared. 'Fess up.'

'I have one sister who I see every few years. She lives in Europe. That's it.' His body was rigid and Halley hadn't missed the sterile way he spoke of his one and only sibling.

'And your parents?' She could tell she was pushing it but she wanted to know. In the short time she'd known him Max Pearson had become an enigma to her and one she wanted to know more about.

'Divorced when I was eleven.' He indicated and turned onto a gravel road. The sound of gravel against the tyres created a deafening noise, effectively silencing any other conversation they might have had. Halley had a feeling that, gravel road or not, Max didn't want to talk about his family any more. The small insight into his family had told her a lot about him.

They drove along the gravel road for a while before turning onto a long, flat dirt track.

'At least it's not as bumpy as Clarabelle's. I don't think I could sustain another bump on the head.' Then again, if she did hit her head, Max would need to take another close look at her. Let it go, she told herself immediately. You may be attracted to Max but he's got too much baggage for you to sort through. Apart from which, Halley Ryan, he's *engaged*.

After her brief lecture to herself, Halley felt back in control of her emotions.

They visited three more patients before the car clock blinked five p.m.

'One more to go,' Max said as they started driving again. They didn't have far to go and he parked in the bay for visitors' cars. The house was a well-looked-after country home, pristine and rather...sterile. They walked to the door and this time Max pressed the doorbell and waited.

'Coming,' a male voice called, and when the door opened Halley was faced with a very good-looking man with blond hair and green eyes. 'Max,' he said with a curt nod, and shifted back on his crutches to allow them to enter.

'This is my colleague,' Max said. 'Dr Ryan.'

'Call me Halley,' she interjected.

'Alan Kempsey.' He extended his right hand in greeting but his crutch started to falter so he quickly withdrew it. 'Darn things.'

Halley laughed. 'You'll get used to them. I broke my leg when I was twenty so I know what you're going through. Max tells me you rock-climb?'

'That's right.' Alan manoeuvred over to the lounge and sat down, indicating that they should do the same. Halley sat opposite him. 'I broke this...' he patted the cast on his leg '...in three places when I fell from the Chimney Pots at the Grampians.'

Halley nodded, her eyes filled with delight, and sighed. 'I can't wait to see them again. The Grampians. Beautiful mountains. Natural flora and fauna. What more could a person want?'

'You've been there before?' Alan asked, his eyes lighting up.

Halley nodded. 'The leg I broke when I was twenty was when I fell from Mount Abrupt. Broke a couple of ribs and sprained my wrist as well.'

'You're a climber?' Alan's tone displayed his amazement.

'Ever heard of Jupiter and Mars?'

'Yeah. Who hasn't? Those guys are legends.'

Halley glanced up at Max, who simply rolled his eyes. 'They're my brothers.'

'No way!' Alan was gob-smacked.

Halley smiled and nodded. Max cleared his throat. They both ignored him.

'That means…you're…the Comet,' Alan said with awe.

Halley laughed. 'It's been a long time since anyone's called me that. I've been too busy working for the past four years to do any serious climbing, but during my stay here I'm hoping to get the chance.'

'Let me come with you. I can't drive at the moment because of the cast on my leg, but I'd love to see you climb.'

'I'll see what I can organise.' She glanced up at Max, who had his arms folded across his broad chest. He raised one eyebrow at her.

'Ready?'

'Absolutely.' She held out her hand. 'Otoscope first, please.' She wondered whether Max was going to argue, but he simply reached down and pulled out the instrument she'd requested. 'All right, Alan. I just need to look in your ears to start off with.' Halley crossed to his side and felt his neck glands before bending to look into his ear. 'Still experiencing a bit of dizziness?' she asked, which was a common symptom of concussion.

'A fair bit.'

'Being on crutches wouldn't help,' she agreed. When

she'd finished taking a good look in both ears, Max passed a tongue depressor and medical torch and Halley checked Alan's throat. 'When do you see your orthopaedic surgeon next?' she asked as she checked his eyes.

'In a month's time. I've had this cast on for two weeks and it's already been two weeks too long.'

Halley stepped back and looked at him. 'Who's your surgeon in Melbourne?'

'Brian Newton.'

'Oh, he's good. You're in safe hands with Brian.'

'Another climbing buddy of yours?' Max asked from his position on the sidelines.

Halley smiled at him but shook her head, glad Max felt comfortable enough to tease her. 'No. Brian's just a colleague.'

'I see,' Max said as he closed his medical bag. 'Well, Alan, I think we're finished here. I'll be around to see you tomorrow.' He headed for the door as Halley helped Alan off the lounge and handed him the crutches.

Alan stumbled and Halley stepped in closer so he could lean on her. 'Sorry,' he mumbled, but she noted he took a bit too long in transferring his weight to his crutches. She stepped back immediately and turned to Max. Had he seen? The frown that creased her colleague's forehead indicated that he had.

'You take care, Alan.' She backed to the door, which Max held open for her.

'Sure, and I hope to see you, too, tomorrow, Halley,' he replied, giving Max another curt nod.

As they drove off, Halley waved goodbye and turned to face Max slightly. 'I think you should see Alan by yourself tomorrow,' she suggested, but Max shook his head.

'Why? I thought you might be happy with his hero-worship.' His words were clipped and any previous camaraderie they may have shared had disappeared completely. Back was the man who'd growled at her first thing that morning for being late.

Halley wasn't the type of person to let anything stew. She preferred to tackle things head-on so she said, 'Out with it, Max. What's the real problem?'

'You shouldn't flirt with the patients.'

'I wasn't flirting,' she countered quickly. 'I was making polite conversation.'

'That wasn't how it looked to me.'

'Then you must have been in the wrong room because all I was doing was making conversation with a patient. The fact that we have something in common means the conversation isn't restricted to the polite niceties first acquaintances usually have. I had a meaningful conversation with Clarabelle and you didn't take me to task over that.'

'That was different. Clarabelle's a woman.'

'Now you're discriminating.'

'For heaven's sake, Halley, the man's interested in you.' Max hit the steering-wheel with his hand to emphasise his point. 'A blind man could see that.'

Halley frowned. 'In that case, you should continue with his treatment, then.'

'You're darn right I will. You're only here for two weeks and I don't want you breaking that young man's heart. He has enough to deal with already.'

'I'm flattered, Max, that you think I'm capable of breaking someone's heart, but I'm not as heartless as you seem to think. I also make it a policy not to get involved with my patients. Kind of goes against the Hippocratic oath.' Her frown deepened.

'I'm pleased to hear it.'

'What have his test results been like?'

'Not too bad. The concussion symptoms should settle

down soon. I suspect the dizziness and headaches are more annoying to him. His sister visits him daily and brings him a meal.'

'That's nice. I guess it's all part of being in a close community. Would you mind telling me about the history of the hospital and district?'

'Why? Don't you want to wade through the paperwork?'

'Oh, I'll be doing that as well—I'm thorough—and you'd do well to remember that. I just thought that as it's now almost six o'clock and we're both exhausted…' She yawned, adding emphasis to her words. She smiled at Max. 'I was up *very* early this morning. Anyway, while we're driving along, I'd like to get your take on things. You've worked at the hospital for ten years so your perspective will be unique. So, please? Will you tell me?'

He concentrated on the road but she knew he wasn't trying to ignore her. She waited patiently. 'It was built in the 1940s, after the war had ended. My father and grandfather, along with many of the men in the town, actually built it.'

'The community spirit,' Halley said.

'Jest all you like, but while that building may be bricks and mortar to some people, it still holds memories and stories.'

'If only the walls could speak.' She wasn't jesting now.

'Exactly. I used to go and help Dr Butcher—I swear that was his name…' Max smiled and Halley found it contagious '…at the hospital on the weekends when I was in my final years of school. Once I'd graduated, worked overseas and completed a diploma in general surgery, I returned here and have been working at the hospital ever since.'

'The VDH told me Heartfield District Hospital was staffed by six-monthly rotations from either Melbourne or Geelong.'

'It usually is. Every six months I have a new recruit turn up on my doorstep, live in the doctor's residence, which is where you'll be staying, and pretend to care about the people they see during their stay. When they leave, another one is sent and the cycle begins again. The only reason they come—' the disgust was clear in Max's tone '—is because after six months in a rural hospital they're eligible for a provider number, which means they can open their own surgery and make all the money they want.'

Halley nodded. 'I figured as much. I just didn't figure on you being here for ten years. For some reason that was left out of the details.'

'I'll just bet it was.' He was really steaming under the collar now, and Halley wasn't sure what to do. Max slowed the car and turned into the hospital car park. Her own Jaguar XJ6 was the only car left.

'And thus ends the tour of Heartfield,' she said as they both climbed out.

'If you get what you need from the hospital, you can follow me to the residence. That way you won't get…*lost.*'

'Oh, yeah, throw that back in my face.' She advanced towards him slowly, shaking her finger. 'I thought we'd progressed past your attitude of this morning,' she said. Max didn't back away but stood his ground. 'And, just for the record, there may only be one *main* road to this town, but when you've been driving for three hours, after getting up at the crack of dawn, the little side streets tend to jump out at you, begging you to drive down them. It was a mistake.' She poked his chest gently. 'And an honest one at that—so get…off…my…case, Max Pearson.'

Max smiled down at her and grabbed the offending hand. His touch sent her senses into overdrive and all humour vanished from her in an instant. She looked into his eyes and saw the teasing light die from his own.

Neither of them seemed capable of moving and Halley wasn't sure whether to advance or retreat. The chemistry between them was alive and pulsing. She wet her lips, unsure exactly when they had become so dry.

Max swallowed and she watched his Adam's apple move up and down above his shirt collar. He dropped her hand like a hot potato and stepped back. Halley shivered, not because she was cold but from what had just transpired.

'I need to get a few things myself.' With that, he stalked off towards the after-hours entrance and unlocked the door. Halley followed him. When he'd touched her earlier to examine her head, she'd thought she'd been imagining the attraction between them, but now the answer was a definite, resounding *yes*. There *was* something between them—but what? Where could it possibly go?

Max was an engaged man!

CHAPTER THREE

THEY didn't say much to each other as they collected the things they needed from their offices and climbed into their respective cars. Halley started to feel a little uncomfortable with the way Max made her feel.

It's just because you haven't had a boyfriend in quite a while, she told herself as she kept the four-wheel-drive's taillights in view. So the first handsome male you meet you're bound to feel drawn towards. But even as she thought the words to herself, Halley knew it wasn't true. She'd met plenty of good-looking men over in the United Kingdom, where she'd been working for the past two years. None of them had set off sparks deep within her. Max did, and she'd known him for less than twenty-four hours!

He stopped a few blocks away from the hospital and pulled into a driveway. Halley pulled in behind him, wondering why he was driving the car all the way into the garage. Surely she should have gone first as she was the one staying here.

He climbed out and walked towards her. Halley cut the engine but he shook his head and indicated that she should wind down her window. He bent down but didn't lean on the car. 'There's another driveway on the opposite side. Park there,' he said pointing in the direction she should go.

Halley did as she was told, realising that the old stone house had been converted into a duplex. She felt prickles of apprehension tingle down her spine as she gathered her things from the car and walked towards Max. He was standing on the front verandah, waiting beside an open front door.

'This side is yours and that side is mine,' he said matter-of-factly as he walked in and switched on the light.

She hesitantly followed him in, the full force of the situation hitting her with a wave of hysteria. She was going to be living within a paper-thin wall thickness of Max! She had hoped, given her unbidden response to him today, to get as far away as possible from him in the evenings so she could keep her objectivity. Halley shook her head slightly as she looked around.

'As you can see, furniture is provided, and I believe a few of the ladies have left some food.' He turned to look at her and she realised he was waiting for her to say something.

'That's nice,' she offered.

He shrugged. 'They do it for all the doctors who come here. The community has a theory that if they're super-nice to the doctors, maybe they just might stay.'

Halley forced a laugh. 'Then, after today's fiasco at the clinic, at least I know where I stand.'

'Ah, now, you're different.' A slow smile spread across Max's face. 'You might decide to close their hospital. You can't expect them to be completely comfortable with that idea.'

'No. Especially when the shire president has been rallying them against me.'

His smile disappeared. 'I'm sorry about that. I did try to put a stop to it.'

'Never mind. It's done. I've survived worse.' She took a deep breath and deposited her briefcase and files on the kitchen table. Heading over to the kitchen cupboards, she opened each one and checked the contents of the refrigerator. 'Wow. When they provide food, they provide *food*!'

Halley took a chocolate cake from the fridge, an indulgent smile on her face. 'Want some?' She placed it on the bench and went in search of some forks.

'Now?'

'Why not?'

He gave her a sceptical look. 'Were you listening when I mentioned a balanced diet today at lunch?'

Halley pulled out two forks, offering one to Max. He declined, but she wasn't about to let his words distract her from her purpose. After everything that had happened today she deserved a treat, and this was just the thing.

'I was listening,' she said. 'I even agreed with you.' She dug the fork into the rich, moist cake and cut downwards, gathering a piece on the end of the tines. 'Trust me, I don't eat like this all the time—just when I need a bit of comfort.' With glee, Halley opened her mouth and closed her eyes, savouring the taste of the cake. 'Mmm.' She slowly rolled the delicious morsel around in her mouth before swallowing and opening her eyes.

When she did, they opened wider than they had before. A woman was standing next to Max with her hand resting possessively on his arm. She had shoulder-length blonde hair, blue eyes and was dressed in a tweed skirt and knit top. Her heavy winter coat was draped carefully over her arm. Christina!

Refusing to feel embarrassed or intimidated—while deep down inside she felt both—Halley forced a smile. 'Hello. You must be Christina.'

The other woman seemed surprised. 'Yes.'

Halley put the fork down and extended her hand. 'Halley Ryan.' They shook hands politely. 'I met your grandmother today. She's a lovely lady.'

'Yes, she is.'

'She has a nice comfortable home,' Halley remarked, trying to start some chit-chat.

'Yes.'

'I also enjoyed meeting her dogs.'

Christina shivered involuntarily. 'I wish she'd get rid of them, but she says they keep her company.'

'You don't like dogs?'

'Not particularly.' Christina's tone was slightly edgy. Halley thought she'd better make amends in case Max's fiancée thought she was insulting her.

'Can I tempt you to join me in some chocolate cake?'

'No, thank you. I don't like to eat between meals. Speaking of which...' Christina turned her attention to Max '...we'd better be going, dear. I don't want dinner to be ruined.' She picked a bit of imaginary fluff from Max's shirt before smoothing the area down.

'Halley and I have a few things to go over regarding the hospital. The evaluation,' he clarified, and Christina nodded, her free hand fidgeting with the pearls at her neck. This was news to Halley.

'It was nice to meet you,' Christina said, and Halley forced a smile again. She watched as Christina gently tried to urge Max out of the room. He wasn't to be moved.

'Would you like to join us for dinner?' he asked.

Halley shook her head, noticing Christina's slight grimace at her fiancé's words. 'Thanks, but I think I'll just settle down with my chocolate cake and do a bit of unpacking until it's time to work,' she said, indicating the cake in question. 'See you then,' she offered.

Max didn't smile but simply nodded before turning and leaving her alone. Once the front door had closed firmly behind them, Halley's shoulders slumped forward in relief. She picked the cake and fork up and carried it into the living-room. Furnished, yes, and very sparsely, too. Then again, what did she expect when doctors only stayed here for six months at a stretch? She herself would only be here for another twelve days.

Halley slumped down into the chair and gazed unseeingly out the window. She heard Max's vehicle engine rev into life and was thankful she didn't have to listen to Max's and Christina's muted sounds through the wall. She'd lived in a duplex before and knew the drawbacks far too well.

It was strange that he hadn't mentioned working tonight earlier. Did he have an ulterior motive? Did Christina still live with her father and therefore Max needed an excuse to get away? Halley frowned, puzzled by the couple. Christina wasn't the sort of woman Halley would have picked for Max. Then again, what did she know about him? Apart from the fact that he was tall, dark and handsome with an underlying sense of humour that she found intriguing, Halley knew nothing about him.

Except that she felt all mushy inside when he looked at her with those piercing blue eyes. And her knees went weak when his breath fanned her neck. And she couldn't seem to get the man out of her mind only hours after meeting him.

Deciding she needed a diversion, she picked up the remote control off the coffee-table and flicked the television on, channel-surfing for a few minutes before settling on a sitcom. She had to do something to keep her mind off Max Pearson and his stunningly beautiful fiancée. Why was it that all the good ones were taken?

Two hours later, Max knocked on Halley's front door and waited. He'd enjoyed the scrumptious dinner that Christina had cooked, but he always enjoyed his fiancée's cooking. A few people in the community had joked that he would start putting on weight after the wedding. He frowned as he thought about the wedding preparations Christina had discussed with him that evening. Something wasn't right, but he couldn't quite put his finger on it.

'Sorry. Only happy faces are allowed through this door,' Halley said, and Max realised he'd been lost in his thoughts. 'Turn that frown upside down,' she said, and stood back to let him enter.

As he walked past her, he caught the now familiar scent of her perfume. It had teased his senses quite a few times that day. 'You've changed,' he murmured as he took in her appearance. In place of her neat trouser-suit was a pair of old jeans, ripped untidily at the knees. Her orange T-shirt was unironed and her face was devoid of make-up. Her short brown hair was still damp and on her nose sat a pair of wire-rimmed glasses.

'Only on the outside,' she jested as she shut the door behind him.

Max couldn't believe how beautiful Halley looked now that the make-up and expensive clothes had been replaced. She had an...earthy look about her and it shone through brightly.

'I've just made a fresh pot of coffee,' she said. 'Care to join me?'

'Sure.' He quickly placed his briefcase in the living-room before watching Halley walk, barefoot, towards the kitchen. It was then that he realised the house was warm—*very* warm—and he realised she'd lit a fire in the fireplace.

Max took off his suit jacket and hung it on the coat-hook by the door. They'd had a fairly mild winter so far, but as it was almost the end of June the season had only just begun. He followed her to the kitchen. She stood at the bench, gently forcing a plunger down into the coffee-pot.

He smiled slightly. 'I don't suppose you found *that*...' He pointed to the plunger '...in the cupboards?'

Halley returned his smile and he was once again struck by her inner beauty. 'No. I brought this with me. There are some things in life a girl just can't do without.'

'Agreed.'

She poured two cups and retrieved a carton of milk from the fridge. She poured milk into her cup before jiggling the carton. 'Milk?'

'Yes, thank you. No sugar.'

'Snap!' She also pulled the half-eaten chocolate cake from the fridge. 'I couldn't finish it all,' she confessed, 'but I'm going to have another try. Want some?'

His smile increased. 'Sure.'

'I thought you might.'

'Meaning?'

'That you have a sweet tooth. Like me.' Halley started hunting around in the cupboard for something. 'I've made a start,' she mumbled, but Max's gaze was drawn to her *derrière* as it wriggled from side to side as she tried to get something out of the cupboard. 'Ah, this will do the trick.' She turned and straightened, holding a tray in her hand.

Max quickly raised his gaze to meet hers and wondered if she'd caught him staring. He desperately searched for something to say. 'Made a start on what?'

'The reading.' She placed everything on the tray and carried it down the hallway. 'The VDH gave me quite a bit of information yesterday on the hospital.'

'Yesterday was Sunday.' He pointed out.

'I know,' she replied wearily. 'And it seems so long ago.' Halley placed the tray on the coffee-table and sat down on the floor next to a pile of papers. 'I had to go and collect them from the Melbourne office and the only time I could get there was on Sunday afternoon.' She shrugged. 'Someone met me there, handed them over and we both went home. It was either that or come here without them, which would have defeated the purpose.' Halley raised her coffee-cup to her mouth. Max tried hard not to wince as she slurped the hot liquid. She swallowed, licked her lips and said, 'Mmm.' Her eyelids fluttered closed and for that brief second Max couldn't take his gaze off her mouth. It was full and luscious. Perfect for kissing.

The thought stunned him and he forced himself to look away. On top of the television she'd placed a few framed photographs. He stood and crossed to the set, picking one up. 'Your brothers?' he asked when she'd opened her eyes.

Her smile was genuine and filled with love. Something inside Max twisted. How he had longed to have a member of his own family look upon him with love shining in their eyes like that. He brushed aside his childhood insecurities as she came to stand beside him.

'Yes.'

'So these are the famous planets. Jupiter and Mars. Their nicknames suit them.' He returned the photograph and looked at the other one which was an informal family portrait. 'You look like your mother,' he murmured. 'I recognise your father now from various articles that have been written about his company.' He replaced it on the TV. 'I suppose you own shares in Planet Electronics?'

She shrugged. 'They were a gift to me on my twenty-first birthday from my parents. I appreciated the gesture but signed the voting rights over to my father. I'm just not that interested in the company business.'

'How does your father feel about that?'

'He respects my decision. He doesn't much care for the study of medicine, although he always calls on me when he feels sick. We're just…different.'

'And your brothers?'

She nodded. 'Both of them have willingly followed Dad

into the company business. They're good at it and they enjoy it.'

'So you haven't been forced to go into the plant and see exactly what it is they do?'

'Not *forced*.' Halley frowned at the word he'd chosen. 'One day I had a hankering to see what all the fuss was about so turned up, unannounced, and went on a regular tour. Then I knew.'

'And you don't get any…grief over it?' he asked incredulously.

Halley shook her head. 'No. I come from a family that respects each other's decisions.'

'Except for when your brothers used to make you climb up and get them forbidden things,' he reminded her, and she laughed, the sombre mood broken.

'Except for then, but as I'm two years younger they often talked me into doing things I shouldn't. Mum and Dad always found out and the boys were always grounded. The older I got, the easier it was to deal with them.'

Max glanced at the photos again. 'Sounds like a nice childhood,' he said quietly, before turning away to get his briefcase. Concentrate on work, he thought briskly as he fiddled with the combination locks and popped them open. That's what you're here to do. Work.

He pulled out two neat folders of papers and held them out to Halley. Those big brown eyes were looking at him with wonderment and surprise. Could she feel it, too? This…whatever it was between them? No. It only existed in his head. Halley looked upon him as nothing more than a colleague she had to work with for the next fortnight. Besides, he had Christina.

'Work,' he growled out loud.

'OK.' She shrugged, taken aback by his change in attitude.

He glanced over at the fire, which was producing a fair amount of heat. Rolling up his sleeves and loosening his tie, he pulled the lounge chair a bit closer to the coffee-table.

'If you want to go and change, I can wait,' she said with that sweet smile of hers. 'It's not as though you have far to go.' Halley chuckled and Max cherished the sound. With her arrival, it seemed as though a breath of fresh air had blown into town.

'I'm fine,' he said. 'I take it you don't like the cold.'

'Dislike it immensely,' she told him. 'Shall we make a start, then?'

He nodded and she showed him some of the information she'd received from the VDH, asking him how accurate he thought the reports were. Two hours later, after several cups of coffee and with barely any crumbs left from the choc-olate cake, they'd managed to wade through about a quarter of the material. Halley unfolded herself from the floor, closed her eyes and stretched, smothering a yawn.

The way her T-shirt rode up and her jeans dipped down as she clasped her hands above her head drew Max's gaze like a magnet.

When she opened her eyes, it was to find him packing his briefcase before he stood and walked over to the door to retrieve his jacket. 'Well, I'm glad we made this start,' he said.

'Me, too.' Halley smiled. 'So, are we having lunch to-gether tomorrow? We could do a bit more work then,' she suggested.

'It'll have to wait,' he replied. 'I have a lunch meeting tomorrow.'

Halley was surprised at how sorry she was to hear that.

'I'll definitely take a rain-check, though,' he offered. 'In fact, I can see us having more working dinners while you're here. We have a lot to get through.'

'Actually, Max, *I* have a lot to get through.' He opened his mouth to protest but she went on quickly. 'It's my job to evaluate the hospital and I must make my decision on impartial evidence. Although I appreciate your opinions and your help in dissecting some of those reports, I don't want to burden you with it.'

'I don't classify the hospital as a burden, Halley, and I'll do whatever it takes to ensure you receive *all* the information you need to make that impartial evaluation. From what you've shown me tonight, the VDH have only provided half the story. The bottom line may be financial revenue but those figures have been incorrectly calculated. Using an outer suburban hospital as a comparison for this one, where Heartfield is clearly not an outer suburb of Melbourne, means that you don't have the whole story.'

Halley smiled at him. He was passionate about it and she liked him for it. 'You're a good man, Max Pearson,' she told him. 'A little eccentric at times but a good man, nevertheless.'

Max raked his fingers through his hair before shaking his head slightly. 'I didn't mean to go off on one of my tangents…and what do you mean by eccentric? If either one of us is eccentric here, it's *you*.'

Halley laughed as he took the bait of her teasing. 'No, Max. I'm not eccentric—I just know who I am.' They stood in the hallway, facing each other, and as the smile slowly faded from her mouth Halley felt the charged atmosphere return. What was it about this man that made her want to throw caution to the winds and kiss him? He was engaged. She'd met his fiancée.

Deciding she needed to get him out of her house, and fast, Halley leaned over and opened the door. The blast of cold air as it swirled into the cosy warmth she'd created made her shiver. 'Have a safe trip home,' she offered in an attempt to lighten the atmosphere.

He nodded. 'See you tomorrow, Halley. Sleep well.'

When he'd gone, she leaned against the closed door and wrapped her arms about herself. Was it the breeze outside that was making her feel so cold or Max's departure? She closed her eyes and listened for the noises she knew would come.

His door opened and then it closed.

Max dumped his briefcase by the door, hung up his jacket and walked towards his own living-room. Slumping down onto the sofa, he rested his head back and closed his eyes. If Halley had either inched closer, or touched him, Max knew he would have swept her up into his arms and pressed her mouth firmly against his own.

It was ludicrous. He was engaged to Christina. *She* was everything he'd ever wanted in a woman. She was beautiful, knew how to dress. She was organised and cooked very well. They both wanted the same things for their future. A house in town where they could raise their family. Christina was more than happy not to enter the workforce and preferred to stay at home with the children.

It had been his lifelong dream for his children not to have the unhappy childhood he'd experienced himself. Christina had grown up in this community, she knew about his past. He didn't need to explain anything to her and neither did he need to justify himself.

So what if he'd never felt that irrepressible tug of passion with her? His father had felt it with his mother and look where it had landed him. Divorce! Max opened his eyes and shook his head. No. He wasn't going to succumb to a single moment of weakness and throw away everything

he'd worked so hard for. Christina was punctual, depend-
able and neat—like him.

They were a perfect match.

Three days later, Halley took a sip of her coffee in between
patients at her afternoon clinic. She was tired, exhausted
and grumpy. Three nights of hardly sleeping at all were
definitely taking their toll.

'Tonight you're sleeping in the living-room,' she mumbled. 'Away from the wall that connects your bedroom and
Max's.'

That first night she'd lain awake until the early hours of
the morning, tossing and turning—just as she'd heard Max
do. The walls were no barrier. They were merely sharing a
house with separate sleeping, living and bathing facilities!
Whenever she heard the shower running she could quite
clearly envisage him beneath the fine water spray, lathering
that firm muscled torso with soap.

The last two nights she'd dreamed about him, only to
wake just before dawn feeling bereft and very alone. She'd
pushed herself to the point of exhaustion, wading through
the mound of paperwork until her eyes had no longer been
able to focus. Max hadn't made another appointment to
discuss the hospital's fate and that was fine with Halley.
Spending time alone with Max was something she was des-
perate to avoid.

They'd split the house calls up, each taking their own
car and managing to get the work done in half the time.
Max had allowed her to do Clarabelle's home visits and
Halley liked to do them last so she could take her time.
The dogs greeted her with a flurry of wagging tails and
excited barks and she made sure she gave them attention,
too. Clarabelle told her stories about the community and
Halley enjoyed hearing them.

'I just wish Max would let himself go for once,' Clarabelle had said that morning when Halley had visited. 'His parents divorced when he was eleven and ever since then he hasn't been the same. Very withdrawn and serious.'

'He told me,' Halley had answered softly, and Clarabelle had looked at her with astonishment.

'Max? He told you about his parents?'

'Just that they were divorced.'

'Well, well,' Clarabelle had said with an interested smile. 'Now, tell me more about your brothers,' she'd ordered.

Halley frowned as she glanced at her next patient's file. She knew Clarabelle had deliberately changed the subject and she couldn't help speculating about what it might mean. She already knew that Max was a very private man, and the fact that he'd told her a tiny bit about his past she now took as a compliment.

She stood and crossed to the door, calling in her next patient. 'Mary Simpson?' she said, and a petite woman, dressed in an old brown calico skirt, woollen tights, sensible shoes and a hand-knitted brown jumper, stood up. Halley had read in her file that this woman was almost twenty-seven. Mary looked almost twice that age, her face filled with worry and concern.

Halley smiled brightly. 'Please, come in.' She waited for Mary to enter before closing the door. 'Have a seat.' She gestured to the chair and crossed around behind her desk. 'What can I do for you today?'

'Um…' Mary began, and cleared her throat, her hands clutching her bag as though her life depended on it. 'I've been feeling…a bit…' She stopped and looked away.

Halley's intuition told her there was something very wrong. Max had seen Mary every two weeks for the past three months with either one ailment or another. A sore hand. A sore tummy. A bad headache. In the notes that he'd taken he'd ruled out hypochondria, and seemed as concerned as Halley now was.

Something is definitely troubling Mary, Halley read in Max's neat handwriting, *and each visit I keep hoping I'm one step closer to finding out what it is.*

'Under the weather?' Halley provided.

Mary nodded but didn't elaborate.

'Why don't you tell me about yourself?' she asked. 'Have you lived in this community long?'

Mary shook her head slightly. 'My husband and I moved here two years ago.'

'Have you been married long?'

'Three years,' she supplied.

'Great. Well, from what I've seen since I arrived, this is a wonderful community to live in. The people are so friendly and there are so many things to do. I wish I had the time to join the quilting group, or the spinners and weavers, or even the rock-climbing group, but at the end of next week I head back to Melbourne.'

Mary's brown eyes widened a fraction. 'So…so you're not here permanently?'

'No. I'm here to help out until another GP is placed and, as you've probably heard, to evaluate the hospital.'

Mary nodded. 'I see.'

'Do you belong to any of the groups in the community?' Halley asked as she settled comfortably back in her chair.

'Oh, yes.'

'Does your husband work locally?'

'Oh, yes,' she repeated, her tone still soft but filled with pride. 'Bernard is the deputy shire president, and he's only thirty-one.'

The same age as Halley. 'So young to be in such an esteemed position,' Halley remarked, testing the waters, and Mary nodded. 'That's great. You must be proud.'

'Oh, I am. My father always told me that Bernard would go places, and he has.'

Halley wasn't sure that being deputy shire president of a rural community could exactly be classified as going places, but at least she was making progress with Mary. 'Where do your parents live?'

'Not far away. In a town called Colac. Bernard used to work in my father's hardware store. That's how we met.'

'Great. So you don't have any children?'

At the mention of children Mary's previous tension returned and she shook her head. Halley was intrigued. 'Have you been trying to become pregnant?' Her tone was soft and gentle.

Mary nodded.

'I see. Let's talk about your cycle and see if we can't pinpoint when ovulation might occur,' Halley suggested, but at the scared expression on her patient's face she realised she might need to backtrack a little. 'Mary, have you been shown how to track your cycle?'

'Wh-what cycle?' she asked, her words barely above a whisper.

'I see,' Halley said again. Taking a deep breath, she picked up some charts and diagrams and came around to sit next to Mary. 'Let's start from the beginning, then.'

By the time Mary Simpson left Halley's consulting office, she had all the information required to track her cycle. Halley had performed a gynaecological examination where Mary had found it difficult to relax. Not wanting to distress the woman any more than she obviously was, Halley had kept the examination short. She took her time writing up the notes, also making a mental note to talk to Max about their patient.

Three patients later, Halley was finished. Wearily she tidied the consulting room, said goodnight to the receptionist and headed to the administration wing of the hospital to do some paperwork at her desk.

She'd been working for at least an hour when there was a knock on her open door. She looked up to see Max standing there, his hands in his trouser pockets and a frown on his face.

'Problem?' she asked.

'No. I just didn't peg you for a workaholic,' he said, not making a move to enter her office. When he didn't say anything further, Halley returned her attention to the document she'd almost finished reading. She could feel him watching her but was determined to concentrate and finish what she'd started.

'Are you hungry?' he asked, and she glanced up, deciding it was best not to even bother with concentrating when Max was so close.

A slow smile forced its way to her mouth and she nodded. 'Starved.'

Were they talking about food or something else? she wondered as she quickly packed her briefcase. 'So, do you want to have your rain-check tonight?'

He shrugged. 'We can go over some of the hospital information while you cook me dinner.'

'*Me* cook *you* dinner? I thought the rain-check was going to be me *buying* you dinner.'

'Isn't it one and the same?'

Halley smothered a laugh. 'You obviously haven't been warned about my cooking! Why do you think I eat chocolate cake for dinner?' she asked as she picked up her bag and briefcase before walking towards him. He hadn't moved since she'd first looked up, and now he was blocking her way.

He peered down into her face, all traces of humour and teasing gone. Halley gazed up into his eyes and her stomach churned into nervous knots and her mouth went dry. 'You look really different when you wear contacts. Tonight your eyes look more brown than before.'

Halley cleared her throat. 'The contacts are coloured,' she explained softly. Still neither of them moved. Halley gripped the handle of her briefcase tighter as she waited for something to happen.

What she felt for Max was a feeling she'd never experienced before. The scent of his aftershave wound its way around her senses, the look in his eyes was smouldering with repressed desire and Halley felt her heart hammering wildly against her ribs as her breathing quickened.

Parting her lips, she flicked her gaze between his mouth and his gorgeous blue eyes.

'Halley.' His voice had been soft and his lips had hardly moved, yet the way he'd spoken her name settled over her like a caress.

Her entire body was finely tuned to every movement he made. As he moved in a fraction closer, Halley realised that Max was going to kiss her and there was absolutely *nothing* she wanted to do to stop it!

CHAPTER FOUR

HALLEY could hear a far-off ringing noise and wondered whether her mother had been correct. She'd always said that bells would ring and the earth would move when the right man came along.

Max tore his gaze away from hers, tilting his head to the side, listening intently. 'That's my phone.' He headed for his office. Halley watched him go before leaning against the wall for support. They'd almost kissed. *Almost kissed!* What had she…he…*they* been thinking? She wasn't the type of person to swoop in and make a move on someone else's fiancé!

She closed her eyes and willed her rapid breathing to return to normal. 'Get a grip, Halley,' she whispered softly. She could hear Max's deep voice as he spoke to whoever it was on the phone. Moments later she opened her eyes to see Max walking towards her.

'That was Alan Kempsey's sister on the phone. She dropped around to see him and he was unconscious, lying on the floor in the kitchen. She said one of his crutches was broken, so I guess he's had a fall. I'll need you with me.' Max was all business and any discomfort Halley had felt disappeared immediately. Their private lives had to be put on hold whenever an emergency arose. She left her bag and briefcase in her office and closed the door behind her. 'Let's go.'

'We'll take the ambulance,' he said.

'The hospital has an ambulance?' she asked in surprise as she followed him out.

'Yes. Very old but still capable of transporting a patient to the hospital. Didn't you read about it in the information from the VDH?'

'No. Well, not yet but I still have quite a bit to wade through.' They rounded a corner near the small emergency theatrette, where they were faced with closed double doors. Max punched in the security code before pushing the air-locked doors open.

'Do you have an ambulance driver?' she asked as he flicked through a set of keys before finding the right one.

'We have emergency crews who not only help out in medical emergencies but also with things like fire and floods. As I'm here, I'll do it. It'll be quicker that way.' They both climbed in and put their seat belts on. Max handed Halley his mobile phone. 'Call Sheena on speed dial hash-11. Tell her we're bringing Alan Kempsey in. He'll need head X-rays for starters.'

'Right,' Halley acknowledged, and made the call. Max drove with caution but fast, telling her what Alan's sister had said. 'If he's unconscious, I guess that means he's hit his head.'

'Double concussion. I'll need to keep him in overnight. Just in case it's not that and we need to operate for some reason, how are your anaesthetic skills?'

'Up to date,' she replied, and then shrugged modestly. 'I did all necessary anaesthetics at the last country hospital I worked at in the UK.'

'Excellent.'

'Oh, while we have the time, Mary Simpson came to see me today.'

'I thought she might.'

'Meaning?'

'That I thought she might prefer a female doctor. She always seems too…uncomfortable with me.'

Halley told him what had transpired during the consultation, and Max nodded. 'I asked if they'd planned on starting a family but she gave me a noncommittal answer. I'm glad she feels comfortable talking to you.'

They turned onto a gravel road and any further conversation died as Max concentrated on his driving. Soon they were heading up the driveway towards Alan's house. The lights were on. As Max brought the ambulance to a halt, they both quickly jumped out, to be met by Alan's sister who came rushing out of the house.

'Oh, Max. Thank heavens you're here. He came round a few minutes ago and he looked at me, but he didn't…he didn't seem to recognise me.'

'That's common, Agnes.' They all raced inside and into the kitchen, where Alan was lying on the floor. Halley and Max saw the stain of blood on the corner of the bench where Alan had obviously hit his head. 'Alan!' Max called loudly, but received no response. 'Halley, do his pulse and BP.' Max opened the medical bag he'd brought in from the ambulance. They both pulled medical gloves on before getting to work. Max checked Alan's pupils. 'Equal and reacting to light,' he announced.

'Pulse is slightly increased.' Halley reached for the portable sphygmomanometer and wound the cuff around Alan's arm. He murmured in pain, his eyelids fluttering slightly. Halley was thankful he'd regained consciousness again. 'It's all right, Alan,' she soothed. She started checking his neck and the rest of his limbs for further broken bones, but from what she could feel everything was fine. It also appeared that his plaster cast hadn't sustained any damage, which was a good sign.

'Glad you could join us,' Max said softly. 'Try and keep really still, Alan. I know your head must be spinning.' Max swapped his medical torch for an otoscope. 'Just let me take a look at what's happening inside your ears.'

'Blood pressure is lower than normal,' Halley said softly.

When Max touched the side of Alan's head, their patient groaned in agony.

'Wh-what is it?' Agnes asked from behind them.

'It appears that Alan has sustained another concussion, Agnes. We need to get him to hospital,' Max told her as he bent over and tried his best to look into Alan's ear. 'Keep your eyes closed, Alan. I'm going to give you an injection now, which will help with the dizziness you're experiencing.' He set about drawing it up. Once he'd administered it, Max went out to the ambulance to get the stretcher.

'Help is here, Alan,' Halley told him softly as she packed up the medical equipment. Halley looked at Agnes. 'Would you mind packing him a bag of the things he'll need?'

'Like what?' the other woman asked, wringing her hands together anxiously.

'Toothpaste and toothbrush, hairbrush, razor, set of pyjamas, clean underwear, dressing-gown—that sort of thing.'

'Yes. Yes.' Agnes hurried off as Max brought the stretcher in. By the time his sister returned, they had transferred Alan to the stretcher and were manoeuvring it in through the ambulance's rear doors. 'Here's his bag,' Agnes called.

'Thanks,' Max said, and once the stretcher was secure he reached out for it. 'Why don't you follow us to the hospital, Agnes? But take your time.' Max took the other woman's hand in his and gave it a squeeze. 'Don't try to keep up with me as I'll be going a little bit faster than usual. We'll see you there.'

'All right,' Agnes said, her voice wobbling slightly as Max let go of her hand.

Halley climbed into the back with Alan and did his neurological observations again. She also rechecked the plaster cast on his leg but found no cracks in it. Max started the engine and soon they were heading back towards the hospital.

Alan started groaning again and Halley's intuition told her that the gentle swaying of the old ambulance wasn't doing anything to help his situation. She reached for a motion-sickness bag and held it ready for her patient. A few minutes later, after turning a lovely shade of green, he used the bag and Halley was grateful for her own foresight.

'We're almost there,' Max called from the front. 'How's he doing?'

'He's slipped back into a drowsy sleep,' Halley told him.

Max pulled into the hospital where they saw Sheena waiting at the opened double doors. She opened the rear doors of the ambulance the instant Max had stopped the vehicle. He climbed from the driver's side and came around to help Sheena.

Soon Alan was being wheeled through the hospital towards Radiology. Halley noticed several other staff members flitting around, doing their jobs. 'The case-notes are over there, Halley.' Sheena pointed to a desk in the theatre preparation area. Halley quickly read up on Alan's details and wrote out an X-ray request for several different views of the skull. At least she could keep the red tape in order.

Agnes arrived just before they were about to take the first X-ray and Max accompanied her to the family waiting room, explaining exactly what was happening. After leaving her with one of the nurses, Max headed back to the theatre-prep desk.

'I couldn't help noticing that Agnes is quite a bit older than Alan,' Halley said while they were waiting for the films to be processed.

'Their parents had Alan quite late in life,' Sheena answered as she came into the room. 'There's at least fifteen years between them, and when their parents died Alan moved in with Agnes and her husband.'

'Does she have any children?'

'Yes. Two boys who work in Melbourne and come home to see their parents every now and then.' Sheena's tone held a hint of disgust.

'Some kids need to find their own feet,' Halley offered, wondering if there was more behind the emotions Sheena was displaying. She didn't have to wait long.

'Finding their own feet is just fine with me,' she said, 'but it's when they seem to completely forget about their parents and don't call them for over a month that it starts to disgust me.'

'Still haven't heard from Marla?' Max asked, and Sheena shook her head.

'My daughter,' she explained to Halley. 'Went to university in Melbourne and I haven't heard from her for over four weeks now.'

'I understand,' Halley offered sympathetically. 'Which university?'

'Melbourne.'

'My brother lectures there. Why don't I get him to make some discreet enquiries just so you know that your daughter is safe?'

'Oh, would you?' Sheena's eyes were suddenly hopeful. 'I don't want to know what she's doing every second of the day. I simply want to know that she's—'

'All right,' Halley finished. One of the other nurses came in with the first lot of X-rays and Max quickly put them up on the viewer. 'It's no problem,' Halley told Sheena. 'Jon would be more than happy to help out.'

'OK,' Max said. 'Now that Sheena's family is sorted out, do you think we can get Alan sorted?'

'Fine,' she replied, not looking at him, wondering whether Sheena had picked up on the undercurrents between them. Instead, Sheena was peering over Max's shoulder as they all looked at the radiographs.

'Everything looks…good,' Max said with surprise as he changed views. He pointed to an area. 'That's where the blow took place but everything looks fine.'

'So I can get all that dry blood off his head?' Sheena asked as she headed for the door.

'As soon as he's finished in Radiology. I'd like to keep him here for the next few days,' Max said, still looking at the X-rays.

'Yes, Doctor,' Sheena answered. 'I'll organise his bed.'

There were several nurses in the community that worked at the hospital as and when needed. All of them were casual, as was Sheena. Max was the only permanently employed professional. The information from the VDH had told Halley as much and she'd admired the way the community seemed to pull together.

Max wrote up the notes and dictated a letter to Alan's orthopaedic surgeon to let him know of the accident. 'Call me if there's the slightest change in his condition,' he ordered Sheena. 'Headaches, vomiting. Immediately.'

'Yes, Doctor,' she responded, and placed her hand on his arm. 'Go and talk to Agnes and then go home, Max. You, too, Halley,' she said. 'You both look worn out. We need everyone rested and refreshed for Saturday's Christmas dinner.'

'Of course,' Max said, his tone dry, as though the dinner wasn't that important to him. He turned to face Halley. 'You can go on home if you like. I'll take care of Agnes and wait until Alan's completely settled.'

She looked at Sheena, who nodded her agreement, before looking at Max again. Was he trying to get rid of her? It appeared so. She nodded. Perhaps it was better that she leave now, before Max. It would give her time to shower and get ready for bed without listening to every little sound that he made when he arrived home.

'Sure. Let me know if you need me,' she said, and couldn't believe the way she choked on the last few words. She cleared her throat, feeling a faint blush tinge her cheeks. 'Goodnight,' she said, not able to meet his gaze. She turned quickly and walked out, remembering to stop at her office to collect her bag and briefcase before heading out to her car.

So much for having dinner together, she thought when she arrived back at the duplex. 'Probably for the best,' she whispered as she walked wearily to her door, pushed it open and dumped her bags gratefully on the floor. She rested against the door for a few minutes, her head starting to pound with the beginning of a headache.

Leaving her bags where they'd fallen, she walked into the living-room and slumped down onto the sofa. She shifted around a bit before deciding that as it wasn't too comfortable to sit on, there was no way she'd be able to sleep on it tonight—and she desperately needed to sleep!

'There's only one thing for it,' she told herself, and half an hour later she'd finished moving the furniture around. The bed was now in the living-room and the living-room furniture was in her bedroom. 'It's just until the end of next week,' she told the inanimate objects. 'Right now, though, it's time for me to shower before getting a *good* night's sleep.'

*   *   *

It was hours before Max got home that night, and even then it was only because Sheena had kicked him out of the hospital.

He'd spoken to Agnes, who'd decided to sleep at the hospital in case her brother needed her. He'd waited until Alan had been settled in with the nursing staff fussing over their only patient.

He'd returned to his office and put in at least an hour's worth of work before going back to check on Alan. Everything seemed fine.

'Will you *please* go home?' Sheena had begged when he'd stayed for another half-hour, simply chatting to the staff. 'You're dead on your feet, Max, and you have a clinic in Riverdam to attend tomorrow morning. Now go.' Sheena had collected his briefcase where he'd left it by her desk, handed it to him and escorted him to the front of the hospital. 'Goodnight, Doctor,' she'd said in her best matronly tone.

He'd told himself the only reason he'd stayed at the hospital had been out of concern for Alan, but as he unlocked his front door some time just after midnight Max acknowledged the truth. He couldn't go another night listening to the sounds of Halley moving about in the other duplex. The woman was driving him insane and he'd only known her for four days. It felt like a lifetime.

She'd fitted perfectly into country life, and after people had got over their initial reaction when they'd discovered she was the one evaluating their hospital they'd welcomed her with open arms. None of the other general practitioners who'd come here for six months had been welcomed this warmly. Oh, sure, some of them had settled into the community life but none had ever shown signs of fitting in—*really* fitting in. Not the way Halley did.

Max moved quietly through his house, switching the kettle on and pulling off his tie. He'd become accustomed to having noise coming from the duplex next door as whatever GP had come for the six-monthly rotation had stayed in the accommodation. Plenty of them had been females...but none had been Halley.

Max groaned and walked into his bedroom. He fell down onto the bed and lay there. The walls were so thin that for the past three nights he'd hardly slept a wink. He'd been able to hear every little move Halley had made.

He knew that just before three a.m. she'd get up and go to the bathroom, as well as getting a drink of water. Her alarm clock would buzz loudly at ten minutes to six and then buzz every five minutes after that as she ignored it until just after six-thirty. She spent at least fifteen minutes under the shower and liked eclectic music as she often sang a selection of songs. She had a lovely voice, which had washed over him the first time he'd heard it.

These intimate details were things he didn't want or need to know, but he did, and it made Halley more...intriguing. Max wanted to get to know her—to discover her favourite colour, what books she liked to read, what made her happy, what made her sad.

'Stop it,' he growled. This was crazy. He forced his thoughts to Christina, a smile teasing his lips. Christina's favourite colour was blue. She liked to read romance novels, she liked to cook and being a part of the town community made her happy. She disliked dogs and asparagus. He knew a lot about his fiancée and it made him feel more relaxed.

'Christina,' he said out loud, and closed his eyes. 'Christina.' They were going to have a wonderful life together and he'd be a fool to jeopardise that happiness. He breathed in deeply, and felt some of the tension drain from his body.

The sound of a toilet flushing nearly had him springing

out of bed. He glanced at the clock. The digital display read 2.53. Right on time, he thought, and then realised that he'd fallen asleep lying on top of his bed, still dressed in his work clothes.

He sat up, his eyes closed, and wearily unbuttoned his shirt, listening intently to the noises from next door. There was the sound of the tap as Halley got herself a glass of water. He kept listening, waiting for the sound of her putting the glass on her bedside table and the soft creak of the mattress springs. He strained—nothing happened.

Was she all right? He stood and crossed to the wall. Pressing his ear to the wall was something Max had never done before, but tonight he felt compelled, out of concern, to make sure that everything was all right next door.

Nothing. Not a sound was coming from her bedroom. Max frowned and turned, barking his shin on the bedside table. 'Ow.' He grimaced in pain and hopped to his bed, slumping back down onto it. That would teach him to mind his own business.

'Forget her,' he told himself sternly as he brushed his teeth and undressed for bed. Easier said than done, was the reply he received from his tired brain. Unable to fight the exhaustion any longer, Max slept.

The next morning he was pulled from sleep by a strange feeling. Something wasn't right but he had no idea what it was. Slowly Max opened his eyes and focused on the ceiling. Daylight was filtering in through his curtains, making reflective patterns on the walls.

As his brain started to switch on, he tried to figure out what day it was. 'Friday,' he said out loud as the strange feeling intensified into alarm. He glanced over at his bedside clock. *'Eight-thirty!'*

Max sprang out of bed and glared at his clock. 'No.' It

had to be wrong. He reached for his watch that always sat on his bedside table. It, too, read eight-thirty. 'This isn't happening,' Max grumbled as he rushed to the bathroom. He was supposed to be at the hospital *now*. He was showered and dressed within five minutes and walking out the door.

Never in his life had he slept in like that. *Never* had he been late for work. Thankfully he lived a five-minute drive from the hospital, but today it took him less. 'Blast Halley Ryan,' he muttered to himself as he pulled into the hospital car park. Why hadn't her crazy alarm woken him up? Why hadn't he remembered to set his own alarm before going to bed? It was so out of character for him.

'Blast her.' He slammed the door of his car and stalked towards the hospital. His mind had been so preoccupied with her that his routine had been broken.

'Good afternoon, Max,' Sheena teased as he walked onto the ward.

'Hmm,' was his only reply. 'How's Alan?'

'He's fine. Halley's already been around to check on him,' the sister volunteered.

'That's nice, but I'd prefer to see him as well.' Max knew his tone was terse but couldn't stop it. He reviewed Alan who was, as Sheena had said, fine. Max headed for the administration section, ignoring Halley's open door as he strode past.

Walking into his office, Max gathered the patient files he would need for his clinic in Riverdam and shoved them into his briefcase. The clinic was due to start at nine, and if they didn't hustle they'd be late for that as well. He ground his teeth together—something else he hadn't done for at least two decades. Halley Ryan. In just under a week, she'd turned his life upside down.

He marched back down the corridor, stopping briefly at

her door. 'We have a clinic at Riverdam that begins in twenty minutes. We'll take my car.' His gaze met hers, ever so briefly, before he left.

Halley frowned as she stood, picking up her coat before locking her office. What was Max's problem this morning? Admittedly, Sheena had been surprised that Halley had arrived before Max, but he'd obviously slept in a bit.

And speaking of sleep… Halley sighed. Last night had been bliss. She hadn't heard a single sound from Max's house, even though he'd still visited her dreams. And, the one she'd had last night she hadn't wanted to wake up from—ever. She and Max had been together on a deserted island and they'd no problems at all with passing the time until a rescue party could find them.

She smiled dreamily as she strolled out to his car. He'd climbed behind the wheel and was impatiently starting the engine. She quickened her step.

'So…' she said after she'd buckled up and Max had turned the car out onto the main road, '…how are you this morning?'

'As if you didn't know,' he snapped.

'Someone got out of the wrong side of bed,' she teased.

'Don't start with me this morning, Halley.'

'Sorry.'

Silence reigned in the car as they continued on their way out of town. She looked out of the window, feeling slightly hurt at Max's attitude. What had she done to deserve his bad temper? Nothing that she could think of.

'It might help to talk about it,' she offered five minutes later. 'You know, get it out of your system?'

'You want it out?' Max's voice was clear and clipped, his hands clenched tightly around the wheel. 'Fine. I haven't been sleeping very well for the past few nights due to your nocturnal activities.'

'*My* noct… What's *that* supposed to mean?'

'Just that around three a.m. you go to the bathroom and then you get a drink of water. Every little sound carries through those walls. Every little sound!' Max clamped his teeth together, as though he'd already said too much.

Halley couldn't believe it. He was angry with *her*?

'Why are you angry with *me*?' She voiced the question. 'I can't help it if the walls are paper-thin. I can't help it if you can hear everything I do, and just for the record I haven't slept well since I got here either.'

'And I suppose you're going to blame me?'

'Why not? You're blaming *me*? I don't get it, Max. How long have you lived in that duplex?'

'What's that got to do with it?'

'You've obviously lived there for quite a while and therefore you must be *used* to hearing sounds from next door.'

'I am,' he ground out. His tone rose slightly. 'That's not the point.'

'Well, what is, then? The fact that I'm more noisy than the other residents who've stayed there?'

'And then there's that annoying alarm clock of yours.'

'What about my clock?' Man, he was really in a bad mood!

'Well how about the way it beeps every five minutes for almost an hour at the crack of dawn?'

'Oh.' Halley's annoyance vanished. 'Sorry about that. I didn't think.'

Max wasn't sure whether she was kidding or not. Was she really sorry or was this just another ploy of hers?

Halley sighed. 'Well, I hope it didn't bother you this morning,' she said.

Max laughed humourlessly. 'No, it didn't.'

'Then why are you angry?' Halley gazed at him in astonishment.

Max groaned and ran a hand through his hair in frustration. 'Because I forgot to set my own alarm this morning and that's the reason I was late.'

Halley laughed. It was the only thing to do. Here they'd been, arguing about thin walls and how annoying they were, and now he was telling her that he'd *expected* her alarm clock to wake him up. Why hadn't he just said that in the first place?

'Oh, Max,' she said, as the absurdity of the situation hit her.

He shook his head and smiled, Halley's infectious laughter swirling around him like a breath of fresh air. 'Why do you have it buzzing for so long?'

'Because I take for ever to wake up,' she told him unashamedly.

'And what? This morning you didn't need the constant buzzing to wake you?'

'Sure I did.'

He frowned. 'But I didn't hear it. In fact, I didn't hear anything.'

'Ah. No. Well, you wouldn't.' Halley closed her eyes momentarily, deciding how best to handle this conversation. 'I…ah…well, I changed the furniture around a bit.'

He turned his head and glanced sharply at her before returning his attention to the road. 'Why?'

'Why not?' She shrugged, hoping to exude nonchalance. 'A change is as good as a holiday.'

'You've been here for four nights, Halley, and you felt you needed a change?'

'Sure. Why not?' she repeated.

He thought this through for a moment and then asked, 'So where is your bedroom furniture now?'

'In the living-room.'

'I see.'

'I'll change it back before I go,' she promised.

'Did I disturb you *that* much?' he asked softly, and Halley's gaze widened. She shifted uncomfortably in her seat and swallowed the dryness that had instantly appeared in her throat. 'Halley?' The way he said her name sent a shiver of awareness coursing down her spine before flooding tingles throughout her body.

'Yes, Max.'

'Yes, I disturb you?' he asked with a small frown.

'Yes, Max,' she repeated, her tone deep and husky. She wished it wasn't but she couldn't help it. Her stomach clenched with anticipation as she took a deep breath. 'Yes, you disturb me. At the duplex, at the hospital. Here in the car—yes, Max.'

'I...see,' he answered slowly.

'And it's quite obvious from what almost happened between us last night that I disturb you as well.' Halley wasn't sure whether she should be saying such things to an engaged man but, nevertheless, it was the truth. She saw Max's frown deepen. 'It's not a problem, though. Why can't we be adult enough to admit we're attracted to each other? You're engaged. I'm leaving town at the end of next week and that's the end of it. Nothing's going to happen. Right?'

Max was silent, his knuckles almost pure white on the steering-wheel. He breathed in deeply before exhaling.

'Right.'

CHAPTER FIVE

SOME things were never meant to be, Halley rationalised as they pulled into Riverdam, ready to start the clinic on time…

Halley expected the drive back to Heartfield to be completed in relative silence, but to her surprise she and Max talked for most of the way. They discussed articles and techniques, as well as sharing some of their own experiences.

'I can't believe we both went to the same medical school.' Halley smiled. 'I'm always intrigued by the way people's paths and lives cross. We could have walked past each other at med school or sat next to each other in a lecture.'

'But we didn't,' Max clarified. 'There's at least seven years between us so by the time you started I would have finished.'

'Oh, yeah.' Her tone fell flat. 'Good point.' She looked out of the window, not really seeing anything before continuing, 'But, still, it's interesting the way people's lives interact.'

Max didn't reply.

'Like the way Alan Kempsey knows my brothers.'

'Knows *of* your brothers,' he clarified again.

'We don't know. Perhaps he's spoken to one of them at one time or another.'

'Perhaps. Then again, as Planet Electronics is such a well-known company, I'm sure there are a lot of people who know your brothers or your father merely from reading various articles about them.'

'True. Do you remember Professor Fitzpatrick from med school?'

'Yes. He was one of my favourite lecturers.'

Halley nodded. 'He's my uncle. My mother's brother,' she added. 'See—it's a small world.'

Max glanced at her before shaking his head. 'You appear to come from a very close-knit family.'

'Appear? It's not an appearance, Max. We *are* close-knit.'

He focused on the road as they hit the outskirts of Heartfield. 'That must be nice.' His tone held a hint of longing.

'It is,' she replied quietly. 'I guess things were quite the opposite for you.'

'Have people been talking?'

'No.' She shook her head. 'I've been listening to what you've said or, rather, *how* you've said it. You have a chip on your shoulder the size of Melbourne, and as far as you're concerned nothing is ever going to move it.'

'I don't know anyth—'

'You're afraid to let yourself go, Max.'

'I'm engaged, remember?'

'I'm not talking about that. You've hidden the real you away for so long, protected yourself from hurt and pain, preferring to have complete control over every facet of your life.'

'What's so wrong with that?'

'Nothing…I guess. Unless it makes you miserable.'

'I'm not miserable.'

'I never said you were.'

'You implied it,' he accused.

'And from your reaction I've obviously hit a nerve,' she

countered. 'I can't help it if I come from a loving and caring family. All I'm saying is that it's up to us to make a difference in our own lives.'

'I'm happy,' he said with a scowl.

'Hmm,' she replied, mimicking his tone exactly. The corners of her lips twitched and she found it hard to repress her laughter.

'So now you're laughing at me?'

'Oh, Max. You sit there with a scowl on your face and your hands clenched tightly around the wheel telling me you're happy. Yeah, right! You really look happy, too!' Halley stopped laughing. 'It was just the…contradiction that I found funny, Max.' Her tone softened. 'Not you.'

They were driving through town and Halley expected Max to slow down when they came to the hospital. Instead, he drove straight past it.

'Where are we going?'

'Do you have money on you today?' he asked.

'Yes.' Halley frowned slightly.

'Good. Then you can buy me lunch—because I missed breakfast and I'm starving.' He pulled up outside the bakery and parked the car. 'I'm really hungry,' he said and Halley laughed.

'I'd better go to the bank first,' she jested as they walked inside.

'Christina!' Max smiled. 'What a surprise.' He kissed his fiancée's cheek as she slipped her arm onto his. 'Halley and I were just about to have lunch. Care to join us?' He turned and looked at Halley, his eyes twinkling. 'It's Halley's treat.'

'I see,' Christina said with a nod. 'Yes, I would like to join you both. If it's all right with you, Halley.'

'Uh, of course it is. Shall we order?'

They were able to get a table before the lunchtime rush

began, and during the meal Halley started to feel more at ease with Christina. She noticed the way Christina deferred to Max in several instances and often fiddled with her pearls, a sign of nervousness, no doubt. Surely Christina wasn't nervous around her fiancé?

Max and Halley had coffee and doughnuts to finish the meal off. Halley licked the cinnamon and sugar from her lips when she'd finished. 'Delicious. I could get used to this.'

'Eating out?' Christina asked.

'Yes. I'm not a very good cook,' Halley admitted to her in a stage whisper.

'You're not?' Christina clearly thought this was a foreign concept. 'But you're a woman.'

'So? One of my brothers is a great cook.'

'But eating out every day would mean extra calories. Aren't you worried about that?' Christina asked with an amazed smile.

'No time.' Halley shrugged. 'I'm always rushing here or hurrying there.'

'Halley's also an avid rock-climber,' Max added. 'In fact, according to Alan Kempsey, she and her brothers are quite well known in the rock-climbing world.'

'Really?' Christina seemed astonished. 'Rock-climbing is rather...' She stopped and glanced down at the table, fiddling with her pearls. 'Never mind.'

'What? Unladylike?' Halley smiled warmly at the other woman. When she'd first met Christina she'd thought her to be rather snobbish, but now she put it down to shyness. It was clear she'd been raised as a debutante and with a father like Dan—who, according to Clarabelle, only valued women as possessions—it was no wonder Christina was shy.

'Well...yes.'

'I suppose it might seem that way, but it's also quite invigorating. My brothers are planning a climb in the Grampians this weekend.'

'This weekend?' Max asked.

'Yes. They're due to arrive in town tomorrow morning some time.'

'You don't know when?'

'No. Jupiter said he'd call this afternoon to finalise things.'

'Jupiter?' Christina was clearly puzzled and Max explained about the nicknames. Halley noticed that he didn't mention Planet Electronics and wondered why.

'Why don't you both come and watch? Have a look. See what's involved.' Halley looked at Max. 'You may even want to try it.'

Max eyed her for a moment before nodding slowly. 'We might just do that. Now, though, it's time to get back to work.' He held the chair for Christina as she stood, before kissing her cheek once more. 'See you for dinner,' he murmured.

'Thank you again for lunch,' Christina said politely.

'You're more than welcome,' Halley replied with sincerity. She waved goodbye as she climbed into Max's car, watching Christina walk up the street. 'She's nice,' she said to Max as he drove back to the hospital.

'So you're going rock-climbing tomorrow?'

'I had hoped to, yes.' She glanced across at him, noticing his body language. He was tense again. 'What now?' she asked.

'Hmm?'

'You. You're all tense again.'

'How would you know?'

'Because your hands are clenched around the wheel and you're grinding your jaw. What's the matter now, Max?

Am I supposed to check with you when I want to do things out of hours?'

'Well, I would have appreciated it. When we first saw Alan Kempsey on Monday, you made no mention of your brothers coming down on the weekend.'

'That's because we hadn't organised it then. I spoke to Marty on Wednesday night and suggested it. They thought it was a good idea and said they'd get back to me this afternoon with the details. That's all there is to it.'

'So the Planets are coming to town. By the way, do they have another nickname for you? Or is it just…the Comet?' He pulled into the hospital car park.

'No.' Halley smiled at him as they climbed out and walked towards the hospital. 'They call me Halley and sometimes Squirt.'

He chuckled. 'That fits.'

'I thought you'd like it. I can see you and my brothers are going to get along just fine.'

'Alan will be sorry he missed them.'

'Perhaps he won't miss them.'

'I'd like him to stay in for at least another forty-eight hours so he can be monitored.'

'Then I'm sure the boys will stop by and say hello. There'll always be another time for Alan to watch them climb,' she said softly before they crossed to Alan's bed.

'Hi,' he said, his voice a bit croaky.

Halley smiled at their patient. 'Feeling any better today?'

Alan forced a smile. 'My head is pounding and every time I move I'm not sure if it's me that's spinning or the room.'

Halley chuckled and picked up his chart. She perused it quickly before handing it to Max.

'But I'm feeling better than I did last night,' Alan continued. 'Agnes told me what happened.' He closed his eyes momentarily. 'I'm just sorry I worried her so much.'

'It couldn't be helped,' Max said. 'Anyway, to cheer you up, Dr Ryan has a surprise for you.'

Alan's gaze encompassed Halley and she felt slightly suffocated. 'That's right.' She stayed at the foot of his bed, not wanting to go any closer. 'My brothers are coming to town tomorrow.'

'Wow!' After the brief moment, his face fell. 'They're climbing, aren't they?' Halley nodded. 'I don't suppose there's any chance of me being released?' He looked hopefully at Max.

'Sorry.' Max shook his head.

'But I'm sure the boys would love to come and meet you.'

'The *boys*?' Alan gave her an incredulous look. 'Halley, they're both well over six feet tall and you call them the *boys*? It makes them sound so…insignificant!'

She laughed. 'They're my brothers, Alan, and although they're both older than me, they've always been ''the boys''. Mum and Dad preferred that to ''the twins''. I've always been the little sister and still am! If anyone should be indignant it's me. Anyway, although you won't be able to see them climb this time, I'm sure there'll be other opportunities.'

'Are you planning on staying here in Heartfield?' Alan asked hopefully.

'No! No,' Halley replied a little too quickly. At the moment she was counting the days until she left Heartfield so she could get back into her normal routine—whatever that was—and start forgetting Max! She cleared her throat and avoided looking at her medical colleague. 'What I mean is, the boys like climbing in the Grampians so the next time they're back this way they'll be sure to look you up.'

'Oh. So you wouldn't be with them.'

Halley forced a smile, aware that Max was closely watching the interaction between the two of them. She wanted him to see that she saw Alan as nothing other than a patient and that she wasn't leading him on. 'Probably not. Mount Abrupt and I have a history—remember?'

Alan didn't reply and Max took that cue to start the examination. Alan's memory of his fall was accurate so, apart from the nausea and dizziness, he appeared fine. Halley agreed with Max's decision to keep Alan in for the next few days.

Once they'd finished there, Halley packed the medical supplies she'd need for house calls that afternoon before returning to pick up the patient files. The next stop was her office to collect her bag so she wouldn't have to return to the hospital after house calls.

Max stopped by on his way out. 'I'll be at the council meeting for most of the afternoon,' he told her as he pulled on his coat. 'If you need me, please don't hesitate to page me.'

Halley smiled at his tone. 'Don't fancy council meetings?'

'Not in the slightest.'

'I understand that Mary Simpson's husband is deputy shire president.'

'That's right.'

'So he'll be at the council meeting, too?'

'Why?' He eyed her sceptically. 'What are you planning?'

'Oh, nothing. I just thought I'd drop in on Mary and see how she is after our discussion yesterday.'

'She might not appreciate it.'

'Nothing ventured, nothing gained. You go off and enjoy Dan's company.'

'Hmm.' Max's brows knitted into a frown.

'You don't like him much.' It was a statement.

Max shrugged. 'He's usually all bluster. Underneath, he's quite harmless. He's done a lot for the community.'

'Like calling a town meeting to warn them against the person who's going to close down their hospital?' Halley asked lightly.

'That's just his way,' he told her softly. 'I'm sure he didn't mean to attack you personally.'

She breathed in deeply, loving the way the spicy after-shave he wore teased her senses. She focused on what he'd said. 'Don't you believe it.' She laughed. 'If he's the shire president then he's into manipulative politics.'

Max smiled. 'Did he *really* hurt you?'

Halley shook her head. 'No. Just annoyed me. Anyway, as I said, have fun.'

His smile increased. 'You drive carefully.' There was sincerity in his voice and Halley's pulse quickened.

'You, too,' she said, all humour and teasing gone from her tone. They stood there, looking at each other for a few long seconds before he headed off to his car.

'You just can't help yourself, can you?' Halley muttered as she climbed into her car and started the engine. 'You're attracted to the man and, regardless of how many times you tell yourself he's not available, you still can't help hoping.'

As she drove out to Clarabelle's place she thought over the lunch with Christina. She was a lovely woman—'sweet' was the word to describe her best. She could see how Max's primal instinct to protect her had come about. Any person would want to protect the sweet Christina from her overbearing father.

She started up Clarabelle's bumpy track. There was an-other car there and Halley parked beside it, wondering who was visiting Clarabelle. It wasn't Kylie's car and she knew Dan was at a meeting.

'No time like the present to find out,' Halley told herself as she climbed from her car. She said hello to the dogs and walked in through the unlocked front door.

'You're running a bit late today,' Clarabelle said as Halley entered the bedroom.

'Hi, Halley,' Christina said from the chair beside her grandmother's bed. 'Long time, no see.'

'Hi,' Halley greeted, smiling at both women.

'Christina was just telling me about your impromptu lunch,' Clarabelle said.

'It was fun.' Halley's smile increased.

'I'm sorry if you felt pressured by Max to pay for me. It really was so unlike him.' Christina shook her head in bewilderment. 'He's been quite…different lately but, then, I guess he has a lot on his mind with the hospital evaluation and all.'

'Probably,' Halley said, not wanting to delve into Christina's statement too much. 'Don't worry about lunch at any rate. He paid for me the other day so I owed him one.'

'Oh. Well, thank you, anyway.'

'You're welcome. Now, Clarabelle.' Halley put her medical bag down on the end of the bed and opened it. 'How about we get your check-up out of the way so we can talk?'

Christina stood. 'I'll just leave you alone.'

'Oh, no,' Halley said quickly. 'This won't take long and it would be nice if you could stay for a while, too.'

'Of course she can,' Clarabelle answered, urging her granddaughter to sit.

Kylie, the district nurse, had been around that morning to change the dressing and to write her report. Halley had met the fifty-year-old woman two days ago and had liked her no-nonsense attitude on sight. At that stage the ulcer on Clarabelle's leg had been healing slowly but nicely and everyone seemed satisfied.

'Max has told you that you'll need to have continuing treatment to ensure it doesn't happen again?'

'Yes. Max is always up-front with his patients,' Clarabelle answered. 'He's gone through everything with me a few times, making sure I understand it completely.'

'Great,' Halley said as she wrote up her daily progress notes.

'He's such a wonderful doctor,' Christina enthused. 'He's so caring.'

Halley glanced up from her writing. 'Yes, he is,' she agreed quietly.

'I'd have been lost without him,' Christina continued on. 'When my mother died five years ago I would never have made it through without Max's help and understanding.'

Clarabelle reached out and patted her granddaughter's hand. 'He was there for all of us. Dan found it hard to handle his grief but somehow Max got us all through,' she told Halley.

'When are you planning to get married?' Halley asked. She needed to distance herself from the feelings she had for Max. They weren't going to lead her anywhere and, seeing how much Christina cared for him, she should help get her back on track.

'Well, actually, we haven't decided on a date yet.' Christina touched her engagement ring and frowned. Halley was stunned. 'Lots of people have long engagements,' the other woman said, still looking at her ring.

'I just can't understand what's holding you back,' Clarabelle said with her usual matter-of-factness.

'Max's father was a big factor,' Christina pointed out, raising her gaze to meet her grandmother's.

'Max's father?' Halley was intrigued.

'He died a few months ago,' Christina said softly. 'Max was always busy with his father and his patients. It hasn't helped that every six months he has a new doctor come into the community. Now…' Christina gestured to Halley '…he has you here, evaluating his hospital.'

'No time for a wedding,' Halley stated, her tone gentle.

'I don't really mind,' Christina said, a smile returning to her face. 'Sometimes, though—' She stopped and shook her head.

'Go on, dear,' Clarabelle urged.

'Well…sometimes…I just want to get out of Heartfield.'

Halley was shocked. 'You've never been out of Heartfield?'

'Oh, sure. I've been to Melbourne twice and Geelong lots of times but…that was when my mother was alive. Dad doesn't like it when I leave. He says he needs me and it's good for women to be needed.'

'Huh!' Clarabelle snorted. 'That son of mine is too much like his father.' She looked at Halley. 'I had a happy marriage, Halley, but my husband was very much the way Dan is. I think Dan would have turned out better if I'd been able to have more children. A sister would have done him the world of good.' Clarabelle sighed. 'It wasn't until my husband passed away ten years ago that I started living the life *I* wanted to live. I've travelled overseas, eaten foods I shouldn't have, done bus tours around Australia. Ah…' She sighed wistfully. 'It was glorious.'

Halley nodded. 'I know what you mean. Although I was working in the UK, I took the time to travel. Europe is so close and the different experiences help you to find out who you really are. As much as I love my family, it was good for me to get away and I really did find myself.'

'Sounds wonderful,' Christina sighed, her gaze filled with longing.

'You should do something about it,' Clarabelle suggested. 'Ring a travel agent in Geelong and book yourself a trip overseas.'

'B-but I couldn't,' Christina protested. 'What would Dad say?'

'Don't think about your father. Think about yourself,' Clarabelle advised warmly. 'You'll never really experience life, dear, until you take some chances. What do *you* want, Christina? What is it that really sets your mind on fire?'

Christina looked at them both, her face flushed with uncertainty. 'I don't know,' she whispered.

'Then at least think about it, darling,' Clarabelle urged.

Halley's mobile phone shrilled to life and she snapped it off the waistband of her trousers. 'Dr Ryan.'

'Squirt.'

She smiled instantly into the receiver. 'It's my brother,' she told them. 'I won't be a moment. Hey, Jupiter? What's the buzz?'

'We're all set for tomorrow. Marty and I will be down just before lunch and then we'll get climbing.'

'Great. I've spoken to the members of the rock-climbing group in this area and they're all looking forward to it. Are you still going to stay the night?'

'And miss that great shindig you told us about? No way. We'll be there with bells on!'

'I can't wait. Oh, Jon, listen.' Halley's tone turned serious. 'I almost forgot. Could you check on a student at the university for me, please? Her name is Marla Albright.' Halley gave him a few details and noticed Clarabelle nodding as she spoke.

'Not a problem. I'll let you know tomorrow.'

'Thanks. See you then. Love you.'

'Love you, too, Squirt,' he said before she disconnected the call.

'That's nice,' Clarabelle said, still nodding. 'Young people generally forget to say they love each other. Time flies by at a phenomenal rate and it's only when things are too late that you realise you should have taken the risk. I take it you've always been a close family?'

'Yes. I haven't seen my brothers for almost six days and I'm excited about seeing them tomorrow.'

'I would have loved a brother,' Christina remarked. 'Or a sister for that matter.' She sighed.

Halley was starting to feel very melancholy. After checking her watch, she realised she'd better get moving or she wouldn't get the rest of her house calls done in time. Clarabelle and Christina said goodbye, and as Halley drove to her next patient's house she felt privileged. She had two brothers and parents who all loved her. Of one thing she was glad—that she knew and appreciated their worth.

By just after four o'clock she'd managed to see the other three patients on her list. She pulled out her road map and followed the directions to Mary Simpson's house. It was situated close to town and had immaculate lawns. Halley climbed out of her car and walked down the path. She lifted the gleaming brass knocker and tapped twice. She couldn't hear any footsteps and wondered whether Mary was out.

Something moved—she'd seen it out of the corner of her eye. Halley turned her head sharply and saw the lace curtain twitch again. Max's words popped into her head. She might not appreciate it, he'd said, and perhaps he'd been right. Halley tapped with the brass knocker again. 'Mary? It's Halley Ryan.'

Still no response. 'Please, Mary?' She tapped again and this time she could hear light footsteps drawing closer to the door.

'Hurry up,' Mary said as she opened the door and all but dragged Halley in. She went across to the curtains and peered out for a few minutes before leaning back and breathing a sigh of relief. 'I don't think any of the neighbours saw you.'

Halley realised that Mary had been crying. Her eyes were red-rimmed and the tip of her nose was pink.

'Why are you here?' Mary asked, her tone still soft as though someone, somewhere might overhear them.

'I was concerned about you.'

'Well, there's no need.'

'Mary, it's obvious you've been crying. How about telling me what's wrong?'

Mary hesitated before her hands started wringing the white cotton handkerchief she held. 'I can't. Look, Bernard will be back soon and I don't want him to find you here.'

'I see. Why don't you put the kettle on and we'll have a quick cup of tea? Yes?'

'All right,' Mary said eventually.

Halley retrieved her phone from her trousers and called Max's mobile.

'Dr Pearson.'

'Max.'

'Please, tell me you have an emergency for me,' he said quietly, and she smiled.

'It can't be *that* bad.'

'Don't you believe it.'

'I'm with Mary, Max. Do me a favour and ring me when the meeting ends. She's worried about Bernard coming home and finding me here.'

'Consider it done.' With that, he disconnected the call.

Mary came back into the room and looked at Halley holding her mobile. 'Do you have to go?' she asked hopefully.

Halley smiled. 'No.'

'Oh. Uh, milk? Sugar?' Mary glanced at the window.

'Why don't we go into the kitchen and talk?' Halley suggested, and Mary seemed happy with the idea. She waited until they were both seated at the kitchen table with their cups of tea and some homemade biscuits before saying, 'So, do you have any questions about our discussion yesterday?'

'No. No. I think I understand. I have to wait until my…um…cycle…begins again before I can chart it.'

'Yes.' Halley smiled as she took a bite from a biscuit 'Mmm, these are delicious.'

'Oh, it's nothing,' Mary said modestly.

'Don't you believe it. I'm a hopeless cook and I do so admire people who can take some flour and whatever and just *make* food out of them. *Edible* food, I should say.'

'I like to bake. It relaxes me.'

'Does the community have a lot of bake-offs and things like that?'

'Oh, yes. I do a lot of baking for fêtes and trading stalls. I'm part of the catering committee for tomorrow night's Christmas dinner,' she said proudly. 'We also provide food for new families in town and for the new doctors as well.'

'You don't happen to make chocolate cakes, do you?'

'Yes.'

'Wow. That was *your* cake you left in my refrigerator?'

'Yes.' Mary was beaming from ear to ear now.

'That was incredible. I'm a great lover of all things sweet, especially chocolate things.'

'I'm so glad you liked it.'

'Mary, in my book you're a gem.' They both sipped their tea and Halley devoured another biscuit. She could sense that Mary was building up to ask something and waited patiently.

'Have you ever been in love?' Mary asked, just as Halley had taken a sip of her tea. She almost sprayed it everywhere. Instead, she gulped and swallowed the wrong way, coughing as she did so. 'I'm sorry,' Mary said quickly. 'I startled you. I shouldn't ask such personal questions.'

Halley coughed once more. 'No. Don't be silly. It was a good question.' She cleared her throat. 'In love?' A vision of Max popped into her head and she quickly removed it. 'The answer is no. My mother always told me that I would *know* when I was in love. She said it was as infectious as laughter, as consuming as a sneeze and sometimes as annoying as the hiccups.'

'She sounds…nice.'

'She is.'

'Do you have any siblings?'

'Yes. I have two older brothers who, incidentally, will be in town tomorrow night for the Christmas dinner.'

'Oh. That will be nice. I hope they've booked their tickets.'

'Yes. I booked them with mine as it was fairly certain they'd come.'

'That *is* nice. I take it you all…get along?'

'Yes. How about you? Any brothers or sisters?'

'An only child. So is Bernard. I told you that he used to work for my father, didn't I?'

'Yes, you did mention it.' Halley watched as Mary took another sip of her tea. Again she waited, not wanting to break the moment by saying something.

'I've been married to Bernard for just over three years now and…I don't know…' Mary held her teacup so tightly in her hand that Halley half expected the handle to snap off from sheer pressure. 'He's a good man, very caring and thoughtful, but…'

'Go on,' Halley urged softly. 'But what?'

'Well, he's getting a little impatient that we haven't conceived yet.' The words came out in a rush and Mary sighed with relief. 'I told him about the cycle thing but he doesn't want to know. Says it's women's stuff and the only way to conceive is to have regular…you know.'

'I see. How does this make you feel, Mary?'

A sob rose in the other woman's throat. 'I just… I just,' she tried again, but the tears had gathered and were starting to spill over onto her cheeks. Halley crossed to Mary's side and placed her arm around the sobbing woman's shoulders.

'Shh. It's all right. We'll sort it out.'

'It hurts,' Mary said through the tears as the sobs became more intense. Halley's mobile phone shrilled to life and she groaned, knowing it would be Max. She stood and left Mary so her crying would be kept private. 'Dr Ryan,' she said.

'We're done.'

CHAPTER SIX

'THANKS.' Halley disconnected the call and looked at Mary. 'That was Dr Pearson. I asked him to call me when the council meeting finished.'

'But…then…he…'

'Mary, Dr Pearson is your doctor. I'm leaving at the end of next week. I'm just a locum,' she said gently as she crouched down beside Mary's chair. 'I need to keep him informed about all the patients I see but, rest assured, it goes no further. What he and I discuss is strictly confidential. You have nothing to fear from him. He's a wonderful man who really wants to help you.

'Now, I want you to get things ready for when Bernard gets home. You know—cook dinner, bake him a scrumptious chocolate cake. Come and see me on Monday morning in the clinic.'

'I don't think—'

'We'll talk some more.' She took Mary's hand in hers and squeezed it gently. 'You've broken through your own barriers and that in itself is an amazing accomplishment.' Halley stood. 'I'll be expecting you in on Monday and I'll definitely be seeing you tomorrow night at the Christmas dinner.' Her eyes sparkled with excitement and Mary managed a smile. 'That's better. Now I'll be going.'

'All right. Thank you, Dr Ryan.' Mary said as they both walked to the front door.

'You're more than welcome. You'll be fine,' she added before leaving Mary's house. As she walked out to her car, she saw Mrs Smythe at her letterbox across the road, watch-

89

ing Halley closely. 'Good afternoon, Mrs Smythe.' Halley walked across the road. 'How's the arthritis?'

'Still there,' Mrs Smythe said. She motioned to Mary's house. 'Everythin' all right over there?'

'Absolutely. I discovered that Mary made the chocolate cake I found in my refrigerator and I just *had* to stop by and thank her for it. I love chocolate.'

'Do you? Well, I made the casserole that was in ya freezer.'

'Really? I ate that on Wednesday night and it was divine. You know, with all the good cooks in this town, I could get myself invited out every night for tea and not have to worry about cooking.'

Mrs Smythe laughed. 'I did hear that ya'd eaten at the bakery twice already.'

'Then I suppose you also know that I don't like to cook.'

'I'll bring ya around another casserole,' she promised.

'I look forward to it,' Halley said as her phone rang. 'Oh, dear. I'd best be going. It was nice to catch up with you again.' She waved as she walked over to her car and climbed in, answering her call.

'Squirt?'

'Marty?' It was a really bad connection. 'I can't hear you too well. You're breaking—' But the phone had already gone dead. Oh, well. She shrugged as she headed for the duplex.

Max pulled into his garage and climbed wearily from the car. He hated meetings, especially council meetings. He'd been rather intrigued by Halley's call but, as he'd already realised, she had a knack of getting people to open up. After all, she'd woven her magic around him. He'd been surprised at how much he'd told a relative stranger!

He walked to the front of the house and was unlocking

his door when the squeal of tyres made him wince. He turned to see a red Porsche pull up in front of his house. An instant later, Halley's Jaguar came around another bend and into the driveway.

She was out of the car like a shot and racing across the small patch of grass at the front. The driver of the Porsche met her halfway, picking her up effortlessly in his arms and spinning her around.

Max's gut tightened and he gritted his teeth as he watched Halley wrap her arms around the man's neck, planting a kiss on his cheek. She squealed happily as he put her down. Then they both turned to face him and Max instantly relaxed. He recognised the man from the photographs in Halley's house.

'Max! Max!' She grabbed the man by the hand and led him over. 'Max, I'd like you to meet my brother Marty.'

The two men shook hands. Max noticed that she hadn't introduced her brother by his nickname. It was as though she instinctively knew that he'd probably never call this man Mars.

'What are you doing here?' she asked, still stunned.

'I thought I'd surprise you.'

'Well, you did. Jon said you weren't coming down until tomorrow before lunch.'

Marty shrugged. 'I decided to surprise you. What's wrong with that?'

Halley eyed her brother sceptically. 'Does Jon know you're here?'

'No,' Marty admitted. 'Let's give him a call now.'

'Well, I'll leave you to your family reunion,' Max said as he pushed open his front door.

'Hey, why don't we all get together for dinner tonight?' Halley suggested.

'Sounds great. So long as you don't cook.'

Halley laughed. 'There's a Chinese restaurant in town. How about there? We can meet at, say, seven-thirty?'

'I'm not sure,' Max replied.

'Why don't I call Christina and you can both join us?' she suggested.

'Who's Christina?' Marty asked.

'Max's fiancée.'

'You're engaged?'

Halley's brother was clearly amazed and Max frowned. 'Something wrong with that?' He hadn't meant to sound so terse, but he had.

'Ah, no. No. Nothing at all.' He glanced at his sister who merely shook her head slightly. There was something going on but he wasn't sure what.

'So come on, Max. Let's go out to dinner and celebrate.'

'Celebrate what?' Halley shrugged and smiled at him. It was a smile that hit him right in the solar plexus.

'Whatever!' she answered.

'All right, but *I'll* call Christina,' he heard himself agreeing. 'Also, I'd like to have a meeting with you tomorrow morning to see how far you've progressed with the evaluation.'

'Sure, but I thought you didn't like meetings?' she teased, and he found it difficult to stop a smile forming on his mouth.

'Meetings are a necessary part of life, Halley. Eight o'clock tomorrow morning,' he told her.

'Okey-dokey.'

'Right. If you'll excuse me, I have to rearrange my schedule.' With that, Max pushed open his door, leaving brother and sister to continue their reunion without him. He heard them go next door and could hear their muffled laughter through the walls.

Max methodically placed his briefcase in the study, hung

up his coat and walked through to the kitchen as he took off his tie. Switching on the kettle, he sat down at the kitchen table. Usually he changed out of his suit but today he needed to think.

He buried his head in his hands. He *had* to get himself under control. In every word that Halley said he was beginning to look for hidden meanings. Did she really want him to come out to dinner? Was she using her brother as an excuse to spend more time with him? She'd invited Christina along, but was that just a cover-up so it wouldn't look odd? She'd admitted only that morning that she was attracted to him but that nothing could ever happen, so this couldn't possibly be some sort of trumped-up reason to be with him. Could it?

Max groaned and shook his head. He went through the motions of making tea as his thoughts continued to churn. He'd agreed to having dinner with them. What had he been thinking? He spooned sugar into his tea, unable to believe how juvenile he was being.

He stirred the brew and took a sip. 'Yuck.' He looked at the cup and then at the sugar bowl. It was terribly sweet. Realising he'd spooned sugar in unconsciously, he tipped the contents down the sink with disgust.

'Get her out of your mind,' he told himself firmly. 'She's all wrong for you. She can't even cook. Surely that should say something,' he muttered as he retraced his steps down the hallway to his study where he sat down to reorganise his schedule to include his impromptu dinner plans for the evening.

Once that was done, he called Christina and forwarded the invitation.

'That's a bit sudden,' she replied.

'Well, that's Halley.' Max massaged his temples.

'Yes. She's all systems go, isn't she?' Christina remarked.

Max was surprised. 'You picked all of that up just from having lunch with her today?'

'No, silly.' Christina giggled and Max looked at the receiver in astonishment. He replaced it to his ear, trying to remember the last time anyone had called him silly. 'I was at Gran's this afternoon when Halley came around.'

'I see.' So had part of Halley's easygoing attitude rubbed off on Christina? Was that why she'd called him silly? His head started to pound and he decided he was thinking way too much. 'So are you free?'

'Yes. Yes, why not? I'll give Dad his dinner and meet you at the restaurant.'

'There's no need for that, Christina. I'll pick you up at a quarter past seven. All right?'

'All right, Max,' Christina replied cheerfully, more so than he'd heard her in months. 'See you then. Bye.'

Max slowly replaced the receiver, wondering how his well-ordered life had altered so dramatically in such a short space of time.

A shout of laughter came from next door and he immediately knew the answer. Halley Ryan. She'd erupted into his life and turned it upside down. Five days she'd been here. Five full days of walking a tightrope. And the crazy thing was that the unbalanced sensation was starting to become familiar to him.

'You didn't mention that Max was engaged,' Marty said as Halley fluffed her fingers through her short hair.

'Didn't I?'

'Halley.' Marty's tone held a hint of brotherly warning. 'The way you spoke of him on the phone made me think you were seriously attracted to this man.'

She didn't reply.

'Halley. He's engaged.'

'I know,' she replied, a little frustratedly. 'Look, Marty, it doesn't matter whether I'm attracted to him or not. Nothing is going to come of it so…' she shrugged '…the sooner I'm done with my job here, the better things will be.'

'Are you in love with him?'

'No,' she said. 'That's absurd. I hardly know him. It's just a physical attraction, and that can wane after a while. No, the man I fall in love with will be my soul-mate. Just like Mum and Dad.'

Marty nodded. 'I agree with you there!'

'How do I look?' she asked as she pivoted for him. She was wearing a pair of black trousers and a russet top. She looked casual yet elegant.

'Are you sure you're not in love with this guy?' Marty asked again.

Halley laughed at him. 'Marty, if I was in love with Max I'd probably be wearing a skirt!'

'Then I'd *know* you were in love,' he agreed with a chuckle. 'Let's go.'

The four of them had a good evening at the restaurant, and she was glad she'd been able to twist Max's arm. Christina started off a bit reserved in front of Marty, but as Marty was used to putting people at ease she soon started to relax.

Halley enjoyed herself immensely as they all listened to some of Marty's rock-climbing tales.

'Halley can scale a rock-face quite quickly for someone so short,' he said. 'That's one reason why she earned the nickname the Comet. The other reason's quite obvious,' he said with a smile. 'But I'll never forget when she had her fall, here in the Grampians. My heart still pounds when I think about it. How old were you?'

'Twenty, so it's over ten years ago, Marty. They don't need to hear about that.'

'Oh, but we *do*,' Christina pleaded.

'We were out with a lot of intermediate climbers and were about three-quarters of the way up when vertigo hit one of the climbers. He was stuck. We needed to get him down, and fast. Halley was the closest so she hooks herself into this guy and starts to talk him down. They were almost at the bottom when he can't hold on any more and just lets go—taking Halley down with him.'

Christina gasped and Max simply looked at Halley with surprise.

'Thing is, if they'd fallen even a few feet more, they'd both have been dead.'

Halley shrugged. 'The trees broke our fall.'

'She broke her leg in three places, fractured two ribs and sprained her wrist. Took her a while to recover, and what does she decide to do while she's recovering?'

'What?' Christina asked, completely enthralled by the story.

'Her Ph.D. I tell you, nothing but nothing stops my sister when she's put her mind to something.'

Max looked at Halley with admiration in his eyes. 'I didn't know,' he said softly.

She shrugged. 'How could you? I'd like to do a diploma in general surgery some day, like you, Max, but it all comes down to timing and I've been constantly on the move for the last few years.'

'Where do you go after here?' Christina asked.

'I'm not sure. Nothing's set in concrete at this stage—I wouldn't even mind a few months off.'

'Why?' Christina was clearly puzzled.

'Halley's been constantly travelling throughout the UK, evaluating here, locuming there. You wouldn't believe how many postcards she sent,' Marty answered. 'She needs a break from the jet-setting life.'

'I'd hardly call it that, Marty.'

'It sounds…wonderful,' Christina sighed with longing.

Halley glanced at Max, only to see him frowning at his fiancée.

'Have you travelled, too, Marty?' When he nodded in the affirmative, Christina asked him to tell her all about it. The next hour was spent discussing the differences in people's daily lives in various countries around the world.

'That was fun,' Marty said as they pulled up outside Halley's house later.

'Yes, it was,' she replied. They went inside and Marty turned to face her.

'Halley, I didn't say anything before, but curiosity has definitely got the better of me.'

'What's up?'

'Why is your bed in the living-room?'

After Halley's brother Jon had arrived the following morning, all three of them went to the hospital to visit Alan. Halley had to laugh at her patient's reaction to his visitors. Alan was shaking with happiness and delight, like a little boy at Christmas-time.

They stayed for about an hour, talking about different experiences, and both Jon and Marty promised to come back when Alan was better and climb with him. Then they packed a lunch and set off with the rest of the rock-climbing group to the Grampians, a thirty-minute drive from Heartfield.

Everyone enjoyed themselves, especially with the legendary Jupiter and Mars around.

After a while Halley heard the sound of an approaching car, but thought nothing of it as she pulled on her special climbing shoes. She was adjusting her harness when a deep male voice, which she would have recognised anywhere, said from behind her, 'Beam me up, Scotty.'

Halley turned and smiled at Max, her gaze encompassing Christina as well. 'Hi. Glad you could make it.' He was dressed casually in a navy tracksuit and she couldn't help but stare. He looked comfortable, and she realised he'd come dressed to climb. Halley thought she'd never seen him looking so handsome.

She quickly glanced at Christina, who was fiddling with her pearls again.

'Ready, Halley?' a tall man, who had his back to them, called.

'In just a second. Come here and meet some people,' she urged, and the instant the man turned Max recognised him as her other brother. 'Jonathan, this is Max Pearson, my colleague, and his fiancée, Christina.'

'Hello.' The two men shook hands before Jon offered his hand to Christina. 'Nice to meet some of Halley's friends. All right, Squirt, are you ready to climb?'

'That all depends on whether Max is game enough to join me,' she teased, intuitively knowing he was waiting for her to issue the challenge.

'It looks so high,' Christina remarked.

'It's perfectly safe,' Jon assured them. 'You're more than welcome to try as well…Christina, isn't it?'

Halley was surprised. Her brother rarely forgot names, especially when she'd only introduced them a few seconds ago. She turned to look at Jon and noticed that his attention was completely focused on the other woman. Her eyes widened in astonishment. She returned her attention to Christina, only to find her gazing back at him and nodding.

'A very beautiful name,' he complimented her, before turning to Max. 'So, is that a yes or a no?'

'Sure, I'll have a go,' he replied. From what she could see, Max had completely missed the way her brother and Christina had gazed at each other.

'Ah…right, then. Let's get you into a harness.' Halley led him over to where there were several harnesses and chose one for him. 'This should do the trick.' She held it out to him. 'I'll…let you put it on yourself, but just make sure you don't twist it.' The harness would need adjusting before being hooked up to the D-clamp and the abseiling ropes, which were used for safety reasons. 'Jon?' she called, but received no reply. She glanced over to see Christina speaking to her brother. 'Jon?' she called again, and this time managed to get his attention. 'Come and help Max while I find a pair of climbing shoes and a helmet for him.'

'You're certainly well set up,' Max commented.

'The boys both teach climbing courses so they need to be well set up,' she said with her back to him as she sorted through the shoes. 'Here you go—size enormous.' She placed them on the ground as Jon came over to help out. 'Let me know when you're ready,' she said, and went in search of Christina.

'Wow, your brother is really nice,' Christina told Halley. 'He and Marty are quite different, aren't they? Oh, not that I mean Marty isn't nice—he is,' she amended quickly.

'Yes. They're quite different. As you've gathered by Marty's red hair, they're not identical twins.'

'It must have been so nice growing up with big brothers to look after you. I was envious of you yesterday and now that I've actually met them I'm more so.'

Christina? Envious of her? Halley shook her head. Life just wasn't fair. Halley had the brothers that Christina envied, and on the flipside of the coin Christina had Max.

'Ready,' Jon called.

'That's my cue. Don't worry. Max will be fine.' Halley smiled warmly at Christina before turning to find Max. She stripped off her woollen jumper, revealing the rest of her climbing overalls and a hot pink T-shirt beneath. 'It can get quite hot up there,' she murmured. 'Let's begin.'

Max stripped off his own top, following her lead, and for a brief second Halley found it difficult to breathe. He wore a T-shirt that was pulled tight around his biceps. She turned away from him and tried to control the rapid increase in her breathing. Honestly, she was as bad as a schoolgirl.

You're a doctor and you've seen this kind of thing a million times before, she told herself sternly. Apart from that, his fiancée is less than half a metre away! She cleared her throat.

'Right. Climbing is just like performing surgery,' she told him as she stepped up to the rock-face. 'You need to take things one step at a time and think out each move carefully. As I'm short, you should be able to follow my lead quite comfortably. Foot- and hand-holds are everywhere.' She pulled on her gloves. 'You'll be fine.'

He was standing close behind her, and when he spoke his breath fanned her neck. 'As I'm in your capable hands, I have no doubt about that.'

She didn't turn to look at him, didn't give in to the urge to wrap her arms about his neck and kiss him senseless. What she *did* do was lift her foot, making sure it was steady before stretching her arms up to begin the climb.

'Focus,' she whispered to herself, trying desperately to get her mind off the man behind her and onto the task at hand. Up she went, moving more slowly than usual to ensure Max knew where the foot-holds and hand-holds were.

Max was amazed at her agility and flexibility as she practically swung like a monkey, scaling the rock-face in front of them.

'Feeling all right?' she asked, and quickly cleared her throat, hoping he hadn't heard the huskiness in her tone.

'Uh-huh,' he answered. He was having a difficult time concentrating with Halley so close to him. When she stretched her leg out her climbing overalls pulled tightly around her rear. He'd recognised the desire in her tone, which only heightened his own feelings. Who would have thought that rock-climbing could be so seductive?

Upwards and onwards they climbed. When they were about three-quarters of the way up, Max lifted his leg and placed his foot in a new position. He tested the firmness of it, before pulling himself up, but his foot slipped, sending a spray of dirt falling below.

'Ugh,' he groaned as he held on firmly with his hands, searching for a new foot-hold.

'Max!' Halley couldn't keep the concern out of her tone. She shifted to her right and quickly moved down to bring herself level with him. By this time he'd found a foot-hold and was simply holding on. 'Max. Are you all right?'

'Fine.' He turned and grinned at her. 'Nothing like a little slip to get the blood pumping more quickly.' He chuckled.

Halley exhaled the breath she'd unconsciously been holding. 'You scared me for a moment there. I know nothing would have happened to you—well, you'd just be dangling by your abseiling rope—but still that's scary enough.'

'I'm fine,' he reiterated, and then his smile disappeared. He gazed into her eyes, reading her concern for him.

Now that the incident was over, she had expected her heart rate to return to normal. Instead, it increased, as did her breathing. She parted her lips to allow the air to escape and gazed into his hypnotic blue eyes.

Please, Max, her soul pleaded. Kiss me, kiss me, *kiss*

me. She looked down at his mouth, noticing the way his own breathing appeared erratic. Was it from his fall or the atmosphere that surrounded them?

'Halley,' he whispered, his mouth barely moving.

Her eyelids fluttered closed as the way he said her name settled over her like a caress. A tiny shiver of delight rippled through her and she sighed. Opening her eyes, she noticed that he'd angled his body to lean closer to her. 'Max,' she breathed. The tips of their helmets touched and a bubble of nervous laughter escaped from her. Kissing on a rock-face with helmets and rock-climbing gear on? Impossible!

'What?' he asked, his lips twitching.

'Timing.' She didn't move, breathing in the scent of him. 'The one time we're both about to give in to the…the chemistry between us…'

He nodded and shifted away. 'Just as well.'

'Yeah,' she agreed softly, and took a deep breath. 'We can't stay here for ever.'

'Ready when you are.'

'I think we'll climb the rest of the way individually.' Halley suddenly felt completely exhausted and just wanted to get this climb over and done with. 'It's not much further and I'm sure you can find hand- and foot-holds to suit your…longer frame.'

Having said that, Halley reached up and started to climb again, leaving Max to do whatever he wanted. It wasn't fair. *Life* wasn't fair. *Love* wasn't fair!

They'd already discussed the situation, admitting an attraction but knowing nothing would come of it. Halley climbed on faster, trying to sort through her thoughts. What had she been thinking? Christina was below them and had probably seen the whole thing. What if they'd actually kissed? What then?

She didn't want to hurt Christina; that wasn't her intention at all. She couldn't help the fact that she was inexpressibly drawn to Max—just as he was to her—but, as she'd rationalised before, a physical attraction wasn't the be-all and end-all of a long-lasting relationship.

Apart from the physical attraction, they had nothing in common. Their backgrounds, their lifestyles. Nothing. Halley lived from moment to moment whilst Max was all about neatness and order. She didn't own a diary and Max couldn't make a move without his.

Yet here he was, rock-climbing with her. Surely that was a good sign that he was willing to reach out and try new experiences? He hadn't mentioned, during their meeting that morning, that he had planned to rock-climb, but when he'd arrived he'd certainly been dressed for it.

Halley thought back to their meeting, recalling how professional they'd both been. Saying only what had needed to be said. Except once. He'd obviously been surprised at the amount of work she'd already done.

'When do you do it?' he'd asked, shaking his head slightly. 'I know the hours you work and still you've managed to keep on top of the evaluation.'

'That's my job,' she'd answered. He'd nodded before saying goodbye and returning to his part of the duplex.

Halley was almost at the top now and looked up to see Marty leaning over the edge of the cliff. 'Hey, fancy seeing you here,' she said with a smile, feeling more herself. She pulled herself up and turned to sit on the edge, dangling her legs over as she waited for Max.

'Come on, slowcoach,' she teased, watching with delight the way his arm muscles flexed as he pulled himself up. He used similar foot- and hand-holds to her and was headed straight for her. When his head was level with her legs, he reached out and loosely grabbed hold of her ankle.

Halley simply smiled at him, intuitively knowing he'd never do anything to hurt her, and it was at that precise moment that she realised she'd fallen madly in love with him.

CHAPTER SEVEN

How could she have been so careless?

The shock of Halley's discovery must have irradiated her face because Max instantly let go of her leg and shook his head, misinterpreting her expression.

'I was only joking, Halley.' He levered himself up and sat beside her, his legs also dangling over the edge.

There were quite a few people behind them, congratulating them on the climb—especially Max—but Halley was oblivious to them all. Max's thigh was pressing warmly against her own, his breathing slowly returning to normal after the exertion of the final haul.

She gazed out at the majestic view before them, trying to control the erratic beating of her heart.

'It's liberating,' he murmured, not looking at her.

She wondered whether he was referring to the climb or the view. All she knew was that it wasn't at all liberating to discover she was head over heels in love with a man who was engaged to someone else.

She silently willed her body to respond to the signals of her brain but for the moment all systems seemed to be on overload. She was in love! *Love!* With *Max*—a man she could never have.

She had to get away from him, had to move—do something so she could escape and sort her wayward feelings into order. She'd only known the man for less than a week. Surely it was impossible to fall in love in such a short space of time? Determined to deny the feelings she'd experienced, Halley took a deep breath and called over her shoulder.

'I'm going back down, Marty.'

'Right you are, Squirt.'

She shifted slightly, getting ready to turn and head back down the rock-face.

'Leaving so soon?'

Halley forced herself to meet Max's gaze. 'Ever abseiled before?' she challenged.

'Now, that I *have* done,' he confessed, and she widened her gaze in surprise. 'There's a lot about me you don't know, Halley.'

Oh, and how she desperately wanted to find out. Halley looked away. 'Marty will fix you up,' she said, and positioned the rope correctly around her body so she could feed it through her hands. 'See you on the ground.' With that, Halley loosened her grip on the rope and slid downwards. Bringing her feet to the rock-face, she did eight jumps before her feet touched the ground.

'Wow!' Christina said. 'That was amazing. It took you so long to get up there and just a few seconds to get down.'

Halley forced a smile. Feelings of betrayal were pounding in her mind and she found she couldn't even *look* at Christina properly. She went through the motions of removing the rope, D-clamp and harness.

'Any time you want to give it a try, Chrissy, just let me know,' her brother said.

Chrissy? Halley's eyebrows hit her hairline. To her further surprise, Christina giggled.

'Oh, Jon, you're such a teaser. I could never do that.'

'Never say never,' Jon replied.

Halley couldn't watch this. Things were just far too confusing, and to top it all off, Marty had just radioed down that Max was ready to start his descent.

'I'm outta here,' she told her brother, and gave him a quick kiss on the cheek.

'Aren't you going to wait to watch Max?' Christina asked.

Halley shrugged. 'He'll be fine. Besides, he told me he's abseiled before.'

'Really?' Christina frowned. 'I wonder when that was?'

Halley collected her jumper before walking to her car to change her shoes. By the time Max reached the ground she would already be driving away. 'Unrequited love!' she mumbled as she put the key into the ignition and started the engine. 'Who needs it?' She'd just reversed out of the car park when she heard Jon call her name. 'What now?' she mumbled, but stopped and wound down the window.

'Halley, we've just received word over the radio that there's been an accident on the other side of Halls Gap near the Elephant's Hide. Max wanted you to go with him to check it out.'

Halley parked the car and climbed out. 'Who radioed the information?' she asked as they hurried back to the rock-face.

'The national park ranger.'

When they arrived Max, who still had his harness on, was speaking into the handpiece of Jon's UHF radio. 'Can you get to him at all? Over.'

Static came down the line. 'I've got ropes in the truck so I can at least get down to him. How long until you get here, Max? Over.'

'About fifteen minutes, Tom. I'm leaving now. Over and out.' Max replaced the handpiece and turned to face Halley. 'Nice of you to join us. Jon, I'll need your equipment to get down to this guy. Tom will have a stretcher and emergency kit so, combined with the one I have in my car, we should be set as far as first aid goes.'

'Right.'

People were still abseiling down the cliff and Marty was one of them. When he reached the bottom, Jon updated him on the situation. 'I'll stay here and pack up the gear. You take the van and follow Max.'

Max nodded. 'Let's go. Halley, you're with me.' He turned and looked at his fiancée. 'Sorry, Christina. I have no idea how long I'll be.'

'Don't worry,' Jon said. 'Squirt, give me your keys and once I've packed up I'll give Christina a lift back to town.'

'Thanks,' Max replied, and Halley quickly handed over her keys. Max didn't wait for her but instead headed to his four-wheel-drive. They both fastened their seat belts and he took off like a shot, driving with expertise on the dirt roads. He checked his rear-view mirror to ensure Marty was still following before he said, 'Want to tell me what the big rush to leave was back there?' There was a hint of irritation in his tone.

'I have work to do.'

'Don't give me that, Halley. I know exactly how much work you have and the time frame you have to do it in. It's not polite to invite someone to rock-climb and abseil with you and leave before they're finished.'

'What's the big deal?' she asked, raising her voice over the almost deafening noise of the tyres on the gravel. 'You've abseiled before. Marty was above and Jon was below. You were in good hands. I had things to do.'

'So it's things now—not work.'

'What's your problem, Max? That I didn't stay to congratulate you? That I wasn't there to help shine your ego when you reached the bottom?'

'That's got nothing do with it, Halley,' he countered.

'Then what does it have to do with?'

He swerved around a corner, sending the rear of the car

fishtailing slightly, but quickly regained control. 'Manners,' he answered. 'I guess I expected more from you.' His tone was calmer now and she had to strain to hear him properly.

'What's that supposed to mean?'

He slowed down slightly but only long enough to turn onto another dirt road. 'Forget it.'

'Fine.' She held onto the armrest as they continued to bump along the road, gazing out of the window at the blur surrounding them. The UHF radio in Max's car buzzed to life.

'Are you there, Max? Over,' a man's voice said.

Max looked at Halley before jerking his head towards the radio. She picked up the handpiece.

'Max is driving. This is Dr Ryan. Over.'

'Good. All right, I'm down with the man. Caucasian, early twenties, no ID on him. He's wearing climbing gear but no abseiling harness. Wrist-watch cracked and stopped at fourteen thirty-seven.'

Halley glanced at the dashboard clock. It read just after three o'clock.

'There's a pool of blood around his left thigh and his right arm is twisted. Pulse is thready. Applying emergency first aid. What's your ETA? Over.'

'Two minutes,' Max said, and Halley repeated it into the handpiece. Sure enough, within minutes they'd pulled up beside a ranger vehicle and clambered from the car. Marty pulled up beside them and did the same, immediately setting up the abseiling ropes. Halley wished she hadn't taken off her harness or her shoes, but didn't waste time and promptly went through her brother's things to kit herself out.

Max collected his compact medical kit and was about to strap it to his chest when Halley held out her hand for it.

'Give it to me and I'll take it down.'

'Halley, I don't—'

'Max, I'm more experienced than you and can get down a lot faster,' she said as Marty hooked the ropes through her D-clamp.

'She's right,' Marty said as he started hooking Max up. 'She's the Comet, remember? Get going, Squirt.'

Thankfully, Max handed the kit over and she shoved it down the front of her overalls. It pressed against her chest but the discomfort was minimal and there was no way it would fall out.

Halley turned with her back to the drop and carefully leaned back, taking her own weight. With a jump she was halfway down, and with another she landed on the ground not far from Tom and the injured man.

'I'm Halley Ryan,' she said as she disconnected her rope, ripped off her abseiling gloves and knelt beside the patient. She pulled out the medical kit and slid her hands into a pair of medical gloves. She pressed her fingers to his carotid pulse and counted the beats. 'Airways?'

'Clear.'

'Right.' She pulled out a medical torch and checked the patient's pupils. They were sluggish, which might indicate concussion. 'How far away is Max?' she asked Tom as she pulled padding and bandages from the kit. 'Press this here,' she told him as she held some padding to the man's thigh.

'Max is almost down.'

'Good.' Scissors were next and she cut away the material around the victim's thigh.

'Status?' Max said as he came across to join them. He also pulled on some medical gloves as he listened to Halley's report.

'Tom, we'll need you up top to help pull the stretcher up,' Max said. 'Marty's getting it ready to send down now. Once it's down, you start heading back up.'

'Will do.' Tom relinquished his hold on the padding and Halley changed it over.

'What about his arm?' Max asked.

'I haven't checked.' Halley ran her hands along the bones, feeling carefully. 'Fractured humerus and possibly the wrist, too.' She felt for a pulse and had trouble finding one. After a few seconds, she said, 'Got it. It's very faint.'

'Let's get this leg stabilised.' They worked together, applying a tourniquet and bandage as well as splinting his legs together for stability.

'How's that stretcher coming along?' Max called over his shoulder.

'It's…here…*now*,' Tom said. Halley looked over to see the ranger fitting it together and ensuring everything was fixed and in place. 'Ready to transfer.' He brought it right beside their patient as Halley took the space blanket from the medical kit. They carefully rolled him onto it before transferring him on the count of three.

Tom started his climb to the top of the cliff with a little help from Marty. 'Get him well strapped in,' Max said, allowing Halley to do the ropes. 'Very impressive,' he murmured.

'Are you having another dig at me?' she asked.

'No. No. I'm being serious. That's very impressive ropework and knotting. You're a handy person to have around in an emergency.' He checked the patient's vital signs once more before Halley was done. Tom was almost at the top and it wouldn't be long before they could get the patient out.

They waited for the signal, and when it came Halley said, 'Right. I'll go beside the stretcher and you go below.'

'Agreed.'

She seemed surprised that he wasn't going to argue. He read her expression. 'You're more experienced,' he said matter-of-factly. 'I know I'm close to perfect but I also know my limits.'

Halley chuckled at his words, a smile lighting her face. Max was gorgeous, and what he'd said had been just what she'd needed to hear to recharge her batteries.

Max felt his gut twist in the now familiar way as he watched Halley's eyes light with merriment. She looked incredible when she smiled and the effect wasn't lost on him. He cleared his throat and looked down at their patient. 'Off we go,' he murmured as the stretcher started to move. It was slow going but finally they made it to the top. They settled the stretcher into Tom's ranger vehicle which was equipped for such an eventuality. 'Swap cars,' Max said to Tom as he handed the ranger his keys. 'I'll drive and Halley can monitor the patient.'

'See you back in town,' Marty said as he started to pack up the equipment. Halley climbed in next to their patient and checked his vital signs once more.

The trip back to Heartfield was taken with speed and care, especially on the dirt roads. Following Max's instructions, Halley radioed ahead to the hospital and spoke to Sheena, letting her know all the particulars.

'He'll require transfer to Geelong hospital a.s.a.p.,' she reported.

'I'll notify them and request the helicopter,' Sheena replied.

'Status?' Max asked, and Halley once more performed the observations.

'No change in condition.' No sooner were the words out of her mouth than the patient started to groan. 'Hello? Can you hear me?' she called, and held her breath while she waited. 'Hello?'

The patient groaned, his face contorted in pain.

'I'm Dr Ryan,' she told him. 'We're taking you to hospital.' The patient's eyes fluttered open and he gazed unseeingly at her. 'You'll be fine,' she reassured him before his eyelids came down again.

'Analgesics?' Max said as he continued to drive quickly but carefully along the dirt roads.

'Already there,' she told him as she drew up an injection. Their patient remained unconscious as they left the Grampian mountain range behind them. When Max turned onto the bitumen road, Halley was thankful for the peace and quiet, even though her ears were still ringing from the noisy dirt roads.

When they pulled up outside the hospital, Sheena and her staff were ready and waiting for them. Halley and Max didn't talk much, except for a few nods here and there, neither requiring words to communicate what needed to be done.

'We need to stabilise that leg,' Max said to Sheena and the other nurse who would be in Theatre with them. 'What's the ETA on the helicopter?'

'Another thirty minutes, Doctor,' Sheena replied as they prepped the patient.

Halley looked at the other nurse who would be helping them in Theatre. She'd gone as white as a sheet. 'What's the matter?' she asked.

'It's…*Billy.*'

'You know this man?' Max said, briefly looking up from what he was doing.

'Sort of. We went to school together. He left in year ten. Billy Downs.'

'Can you contact his next of kin?' Sheena was asking her nurse.

'I can check in the phone book. His parents used to live in Bugglebrook.'

Sheena nodded. 'Get someone else to do it. We need you here.'

'Yes, Sister.' They continued to work quickly, knowing that a fractured femur could be life-threatening.

'So, Billy,' Halley said softly to her patient as she anaesthetised him, 'let's get you sorted out.'

Max was able to find the ruptured blood vessels and suture them closed. They stabilised their patient and prepared him for transfer. 'What's the status on the family?' Max asked as he pulled his gloves and mask off.

'I'll check for you,' Sheena told him, and after she'd disposed of her theatre garb she went in search of her staff.

'You're amazing, Max,' Halley told him softly as she watched him de-gown. She was still monitoring her patient, ensuring that he didn't suffer any adverse reaction to the anaesthetic. Max turned and looked at her, their gazes locking. Thankfully, the small recovery area was temporarily abandoned. Halley cleared her throat. 'I…um…mean that you're very good at…'

He nodded and turned to the door. 'I knew what you meant,' he said, and walked out.

Halley closed her eyes momentarily before shaking her head. Depression started to settle in but she quickly pushed it away. No. She wasn't about to start feeling sorry for herself simply because the man she loved was engaged to someone else. She wouldn't allow herself.

But as the afternoon wore on, and Billy Downs was transferred to Geelong for further treatment, Halley realised that she couldn't stop it.

Max drove them back to the duplex at a quarter to six, the journey being completed in silence.

'Thanks,' she muttered as she climbed from the vehicle and headed quickly to her front door. Her car was in the driveway and Marty's van was parked behind it. Halley sighed. Just when she needed to sit in private and have a really good cry, she had to put on a brave face for her brothers.

As she opened her door, she realised her brothers weren't the only people there.

'Hi, Halley,' Christina said as she quickly rose from the kitchen table where they were all enjoying a cup of tea. The other woman fiddled with her pearls and glanced quickly at Jon and then the ceiling before meeting Halley's gaze once more. 'I take it that Max is home, too?'

Halley nodded.

'Oh, well, yes. Thank you, gentlemen, for keeping me company.'

Jon stood and smiled at Christina. 'Our pleasure, Chrissy. See you tonight.'

Christina's other hand came up to fiddle with the pearls and Halley realised that the other woman was very nervous about something. 'Oh. Yes. Of course. See you there.' With that, she glanced once more at Halley before hurrying from the room as though her life depended on it.

After the front door had clicked shut, Halley gave Jon a quizzical look and sat down in the chair Christina had vacated. 'What's going on?'

Jon shrugged. 'We came back and had a cup of tea while we were waiting. Fascinating woman,' he said.

Halley looked at Marty.

'How's the patient?' he asked.

'Oh, yeah,' Jon nodded. 'How's the patient?'

'He'll be fine. He's on his way to Geelong hospital so he's now out of our hands.' She slumped down onto the table and closed her eyes.

'You all right, Squirt?' Jon asked.

'Mmm.'

'Cup of tea?' Marty asked.

'Mmm,' she replied again, nodding her head.

'Chrissy is one lovely woman,' Jon said softly.

Halley lifted her head and glared at him. 'Lovely *engaged* woman, and stop calling her Chrissy,' she told him.

'Why? She told me she liked it.' Halley raised her eyebrows in surprise but her brother continued, 'So I'm not allowed to like a person simply because they're engaged to someone else?'

'Ha! Who are you trying to kid, Jon?' Halley made sure she spoke very softly, knowing far too well how easily voices carried through the walls.

'It's clearly not going to last,' Jon retorted.

'How do you know, Dr Freud?' Marty asked with a grin as he placed a cup of tea in front of Halley.

'I just do,' Jon whispered. 'Besides, you and Max have been making monkey eyes at each other all afternoon.'

Halley smiled. 'Monkey eyes? Don't be so ridiculous.' Inside, she was beginning to tremble. Was she really that obvious?

'Yoo-hoo. Halley.'

Halley turned and looked in the direction of the caller. 'This way, boys. You've just got to meet Clarabelle.' A smile brightened Halley's face as she crossed to where Clarabelle was sitting in her wheelchair. 'Hi,' she said and kissed the other woman's cheek. 'How are you feeling?'

'Wonderful. Never better. Who are these fine-looking gentlemen?'

'These are my brothers, Jon and Marty.'

'Oh, the Planets. That's right.' Clarabelle shook hands with both of them. 'You must come and tell me all about your climbing exploits. I just adore hearing other people's stories.'

'Only if you'll promise to share some of yours,' Jon replied with a smile.

'Ooh, that's a powerful smile you have there. I'll bet it's turned many a head.'

'Clarabelle,' Halley warned lightly. 'Stop flirting with my brother. He's too young for you.'

'Says who?' Clarabelle laughed.

'Says *me*.' It was Christina who spoke and she bent to kiss Clarabelle's cheek. 'How are you feeling, Gran?'

Christina was resplendent in blue satin, the pearls still securely at her neck, but it was the man beside her, wearing a black suit, white shirt and matching blue bow tie and cummerbund who caught Halley's eye.

Halley had to remind herself to breathe as Max's gaze met hers. He looked…downright sexy and she wondered whether she'd ever breathe again!

'Pardon?' Halley said, and quickly looked at Clarabelle, who had spoken.

'I said I'd told you that tonight was going to be the social event of the year.'

'Ah…yes. Yes, you did, and…' Halley glanced around the room which was quickly filling up '…it looks as though you're right as usual, Clarabelle.'

'Halley?' She turned to see Sheena Albright heading in their direction. 'Excuse us,' Sheena said and tugged Halley away. 'Guess what's happened?' The nurse was animated with delight. 'When I got home from the hospital today there was a message on my machine from Marla, saying that she's coming home next weekend. Just for two days, mind you, but she's actually coming to see us. I'm so happy.'

'That's fantastic news,' Halley replied as Sheena squeezed her hand.

'So you don't need to bother your brother and ask him to look her up.'

Halley nodded slowly. She hadn't asked Jon whether or not he'd contacted Marla, but she was sure he had. Then again, he hadn't mentioned anything. Perhaps Marla had come to her senses on her own. 'Thanks for letting me know,' Halley replied, before Sheena left.

'Good news?' Max asked softly from behind her, and Halley felt goose-bumps cascade over her body at his nearness.

'Yes,' she answered softly, looking up into his mesmerising blue eyes. 'Marla's coming home next weekend.'

'I see. Did Jon speak to her?'

'I'm not sure. I keep forgetting to ask.' Halley smiled up at him.

'It's been a busy day,' he agreed.

And one she'd never forget, she added silently. The day she'd discovered she was in love.

'You look…lovely,' Max said softly.

She glanced down at her clothes and smiled. As Halley hadn't known about the Christmas event when she'd packed to come to Heartfield, she was dressed in a pair of black trousers, a cream blouse and a new red silk jacket she'd packed on impulse.

'Thank you, Max.'

'I'm surprised that even an occasion such as this hasn't prompted you to wear a dress.' He smiled as he spoke and she knew he was having a dig at her. She shook her head.

'Sorry. I didn't pack any dresses or skirts.' She cursed the way her tone had gone husky as she'd answered the question, but couldn't stop it.

Jon interrupted, 'The last time I remember Halley wearing a dress was when she graduated.'

'That doesn't count,' Marty joined in. 'The graduation gown over the top of shirt and trousers doesn't count.'

Jon snapped his fingers. 'You know, bro, you're right. Gee, then I can't remember Halley wearing a dress at all!' The boys laughed at their sister.

'Ha, ha,' Halley responded to their teasing.

'But she *has* promised to wear a dress the day she gets married,' Marty continued.

Jon frowned. 'Has she actually promised? The last I remember it was a toss-up between flowing white satin or white leather trousers.'

'White leather trousers?' Christina's eyes were wide with amazement. 'You wouldn't, would you?'

Halley smiled brightly at all of them, ensuring her eyes didn't meet Max's. 'You'll just have to wait and see,' she told them, and Clarabelle laughed.

'Nice to see you young folk having fun.' She glanced up at the ceiling above them. 'Ooh, look at this. I've just realised we've been standing beneath the mistletoe.'

They all looked up.

'Well?' Clarabelle asked. 'Who's going to kiss me?'

Marty smiled. 'It would be my honour,' he said, and bent to give Clarabelle a quick kiss. She then accepted a kiss from Jon, followed by one from Max.

'You handsome things, you. What are you all doing afterwards?' Clarabelle teased, and everyone laughed.

But as Christina also received kisses from the three men, Halley realised what was coming. She glanced at Max and found him looking hungrily down at her.

'Go on, Max,' Clarabelle urged. 'Halley can't just kiss her brothers!'

Halley couldn't move. Her heart was pounding furiously against her ribs, forcing the blood to pump faster around her body. Her mouth went dry. Max was going to kiss her.

Her palms were moist with perspiration. The scent of his aftershave filled her senses. It was going to happen! As though in slow motion, he leaned closer still and she could feel his breath on her face.

Everyone around them faded into oblivion and Halley's eyelids fluttered closed while her mind still kept reeling from the fact that Max was about to kiss her. Her breath caught in her throat but right at this moment in time she didn't *need* to breathe. She had Max!

His lips made contact with hers for a brief yet infinite moment and Halley felt as though she'd been swept up onto cloud nine and was floating away with the dream.

Her love for him grew in that instant. For the past six days all she'd dreamed about had been a kiss from Max, and now it was really happening. Her lips tingled at his touch before a flood of desire burst throughout her body.

CHAPTER EIGHT

'THERE,' Halley heard Clarabelle say, although the words seemed to be in a haze. 'Now everyone's been kissed. Can someone wheel me over to the punch-bowl? I'd really like a drink.'

Halley just stood and stared up at Max, unable to believe that such a short kiss had knocked her world off its axis. It had seemed to last for ever, when in reality it had been no longer than a quick peck on the lips.

Max cleared his throat and then looked up. 'Mistletoe.' He nodded. 'Would you like a drink?'

Halley was stunned. How did he expect her to think or speak rationally after an intense moment like that? 'Ah…yeah. Hmm? I mean, yes. A drink sounds…good.' She followed Max and everyone else to the punch-bowl and allowed him to pour her a glass.

'Excuse me,' Max said, and before anyone could ask why he walked out through the side door of the community hall.

What had he been thinking? He'd just kissed Halley—in front of his fiancée *and* everyone else at the dinner. 'Mistletoe,' he mumbled to himself. Silly little plant, and it hadn't even been real. He'd kissed Halley beneath plastic mistletoe. Whose idea had it been to hang mistletoe around the room? 'Probably Clarabelle's,' he said out loud as he walked to his car.

A few people were still coming in and waved to him. 'You haven't been called away to an emergency already, have you?' one man asked.

Max smiled politely. 'No. Just need to get something from my car.' He waved to them and kept on going. When he reached his car he unlocked the door and opened it. One small kiss. One brief second he'd pressed his lips against Halley's and everything had been turned upside down.

Ever since his mother had left, Max had held himself in check. He'd kept everything in place, including his emotions. He'd grown fond of Christina and had eventually asked her to marry him. Both had agreed it was the sensible and right thing to do. He'd never professed undying love for her, deciding that it was better that way. He'd never be hurt by a woman the way his father had been hurt by his mother.

That was before he'd met Halley Ryan!

He leaned his head against the doorframe. What had possessed him to kiss her? He'd been fantasising about it since she'd arrived last Monday, and even though this had been a simple peck it had only increased the burning sensation in his gut, making him want more.

They'd both admitted to being attracted to one another but they'd also agreed that nothing could come of it. Max ran his tongue along his lips and closed his eyes, groaning in agony. He could still smell the faintest hint of her perfume on his clothes and it was driving him to distraction. The feel of her lips on his had mesmerised him so that anyone and everything had disappeared into oblivion.

It had happened…and now he had to live with that memory for the rest of his life. He'd kissed Christina in a similar way many a time, but *never* had he felt *any* of what he was feeling for Halley.

Max opened his eyes and stood up straight, raking an unsteady hand through his hair. He had to get Halley Ryan out of his mind once and for all. No more touching, no more intimate scenes and definitely no more kissing! He was engaged to Christina. He was committed to Christina! He'd never broken his word in his entire life and he wasn't about to start now. His life with Christina would be calm and orderly with no surprises, which was just the way he preferred his life to be. Christina was the sensible choice for a wife.

Max closed the door to his car and locked it, straightened his bow tie and gave a brief tug to the lapels of his jacket. After giving himself a nod of encouragement, he headed back towards the hall.

'Max? Oh, Max, there you are,' Christina said as she came outside. 'I was looking for you.' She slipped her arm through his, just as she always did. Max briefly placed his hand on top and gave her fingers a pat. 'They're ready to start the evening.'

The evening progressed without a hitch and, as Clarabelle had predicted, the food was marvellous. Halley sat between her two brothers, across the table from Max and Christina. The seating arrangements made it difficult not to look at him as he was directly in her line of vision, but as the night progressed he appeared to relax a little.

She guessed that the unplanned reaction they'd had to each other had sent his neat, ordered world into a tail-spin. It had taken him until after the main course before he'd been able to look her directly in the eye and smile. In some ways, she wished he hadn't. The way the corners of his mouth turned up and the twinkle of amusement in his gorgeous eyes made Halley sparkle deep within, knocking her for another six.

Marty called her name, bringing her back to the present, and she turned to give her brother her full attention.

Mary Simpson was helping to serve the meals and Halley remembered that she was part of the committee. Halley smiled brightly at Mary, who'd seemed rather nervous when she'd brought the first course, but now, as she brought the desserts around, she was smiling brightly, obviously happy with the way things were going.

When they'd finished dessert, Max took her over to where Dan was standing, talking to his deputy shire president. Mary was with her husband and her face registered her despair. Halley wanted to reach out and protect her, to reassure her that she would *never* say anything to Bernard about Mary's problems unless Mary had authorised her to.

Bernard was a bit reserved towards Halley, probably because of what Dan had said during the town meeting before her arrival. When the introductions had been made, Dan looked menacingly at Halley. 'Closing our hospital yet?'

Mary seemed even more agitated at Dan's attitude, and she quickly excused herself, saying she was needed in the kitchen to help with the washing-up. Dan glared at Halley, as though she should go with Mary to her 'rightful place'— the kitchen.

Halley took a deep breath and smiled sweetly at him. She opened her mouth to speak, but Max beat her to it.

'No verdict as yet, Dan,' he said with a forced smile. 'Halley and I still have a few more files to sort through.'

Christina came over with Jon and Marty in tow, capturing her father's attention. 'Dad, I'd like you to meet some new friends of mine. Martin and Jonathan.'

Dan shook hands with both men, frowning slightly as he did so. 'You both look...familiar.'

'Well, I suppose it's because they're Halley's—'

'Of course,' Dan interrupted. 'Planet Electronics. I read an article just yesterday in a business magazine about the two of you.'

Both of her brothers nodded and smiled. Christina seemed stunned. She glanced at Halley.

'Something wrong?' Halley whispered.

'Planet Electronics?' Christina eyes were wide with disbelief. 'You…you never said.'

'Said what?' Halley was puzzled.

'What does *she* have to do with it?' Dan asked, his rude attitude making her brothers bristle.

'Halley is their sister, Dad,' Christina told him.

Dan's eyes widened in horror. 'You're Jack Ryan's daughter?'

'Yes.' Halley knew Dan was remembering everything he'd said to her and how he'd basically urged the community to turn against her when she'd arrived.

'But you're a doctor?'

'Yes,' Halley said slowly, as though she were speaking to an imbecile.

'You don't need to be. You're rich.'

She forced a smile, unable to believe a man could be so tacky. Jon put his arm around her.

'We're all very proud of our Halley,' he said, and Marty agreed.

'Stepping out on her own. Doing her own thing. Finding what she was passionate about.' He squeezed her shoulder. 'Yes. We're all *very* proud of *our* doctor.'

Dan simply stuttered at hearing Jon extol Halley's worth, and it was all she could do not to smile. 'Oh, well…yes. Yes…of course.'

'Excuse me,' she said, clearing her throat. 'I need to go…freshen up.'

'I'll come, too,' Christina said, and looped her arm through Halley's. 'I had no idea,' she whispered as they headed towards the ladies' room.

Halley heard Dan saying, 'I approached your father once, about setting up something here in Heartfield…' Halley was glad she was leaving. It appeared that Jon and Marty were about to get a business proposal. Then again, it wouldn't

be the first time something like that had happened. She felt
secure in the knowledge that her brothers were experienced
in dealing with people like Dan.

Halley returned her attention to Christina, who was gripping her arm rather tightly. 'So you didn't know my family
was Planet Electronics?'

'Not a clue.'

'Why is it so important?'

'Oh… It isn't. It's just that, well…' Christina stopped
and looked around them. 'Come outside for a minute.'

As Halley's arm was still in Christina's grip, she had no
option but to go. 'Christina?'

'Oh, Halley,' she said as she frantically looked around
in case they were overheard. She dropped Halley's arm and
fiddled with her pearls. Something wasn't right, and Halley
was starting to feel uneasy. 'I can't believe that Jon
is…who he is.'

'Jon? This is about Jon?'

'Oh…no,' she quickly denied, but Halley wasn't sure she
believed her. 'It's just that—well, it's my background, I
guess. After my mother died, my father became, well,
more…authoritarian. I mean, I'm twenty-nine years old and
I still live at home and look after my father. I *really* miss
my mum and wish she was here for me to talk to. Oh, I've
got Gran, and she's great, but it's…well, it's not the same.
Dad's never encouraged me to…you know, have a job or
anything. He told me that I was destined to be a wife and
mother who was involved in charity work, just like my
mother was. It was good enough for her so…' Christina
shrugged, not finishing her sentence. 'Gran keeps telling
me to do whatever I want and not to listen to my father,
but I just…can't.'

'Because you're not sure how?'

'Yes.' Christina brought her other hand up to the pearls. 'These were my mother's.'

Halley nodded, realising the other woman's problems. Christina was lost in the wilderness of life and wasn't quite sure how to find her way out. 'They make you feel close to her?'

'Yes. When I first met you, I wasn't sure I liked you. My father had been saying that we shouldn't make you feel welcome and Max had been disagreeing with him. I wasn't sure *what* to believe. Max has always been there for me. For as long as I can remember. He was wonderful when my mother died, and whenever he came to tea he was always so charming and polite. He makes me feel...' She searched for the right word.

Halley wasn't sure she wanted to hear this. Her own feelings for Max ran so deep, so true. To stand here and listen to the woman who wore his ring profess her love for the man was almost more than Halley could bear. Then again, it appeared Christina didn't have a lot of friends she could talk to, and Halley counted herself fortunate to be put into that category.

'Safe,' she finally came up with. 'I love him,' she said matter-of-factly. 'I truly do. But...I don't know. Isn't there...*more*?'

Halley frowned. 'More *what*?'

'More...I don't know...fireworks? More...feeling, more intensity?' Christina looked down at her hands and then back at Halley. 'Seeing you and your brothers together has made me realise what I *really* feel for Max. I look upon him as the big brother I've never had.'

Halley was stunned. Surely Christina didn't realise what she was saying. Halley shook her head as though to clear the words away.

'There you two are,' Max said from the doorway.

'Santa's about to arrive. Come inside before you both catch colds.'

Halley's nerves were as tight as a drum and Max's un-announced appearance didn't help to appease them. How long had he been standing there? How much had he heard? She found it hard to meet his gaze as both she and Christina went inside.

'Halley.' Max placed his hand on her shoulder as she went to walk past him. Christina had gone on ahead into the hall. 'I'm sorry,' he said softly. 'I'm sorry for the way Dan treated you.'

'It's not your fault.'

They stood in the small corridor, their bodies almost pressed together. Halley flattened herself against the wall, her gaze focused on his bow tie. Only a few hours ago his lips had been pressed to her own, and even though she'd vowed not to think of it again here she was, breaking her vow.

Slowly, her gaze lifted to rest on his lips. He wasn't smiling. Her eyes flicked up to his to find them filled with desire and longing.

'Halley,' he whispered.

Butterflies came to life in her stomach and they fluttered around nervously. Her knees grew weak just from the way he was gazing down at her. Halley had no idea what she should do. She knew what she *wanted* to do, but there was no way she'd ever do it.

Halley sighed and shook her head sadly from side to side. 'We can't do this, Max.' Her words were barely audible but she knew from the way that Max nodded his head slightly that he agreed with her. 'It'll tear us both apart.'

'I know.'

He made no effort to touch her but Halley felt the caress from his entire body. A relationship founded on physical attraction couldn't possibly last, especially when one person was engaged to someone else.

'I made a commitment.'

Halley felt a lump in her throat and found herself unable to speak, so she just nodded. She admired his honour in staying with Christina.

A loud crash from the kitchen broke the mood between them. They both rushed in the direction of the sound, and when Halley opened the door to the kitchen it was to see Mary sitting on the floor with broken crockery all around her.

'Stand back,' Max ordered calmly, as some of the other women came over to help Mary up. 'Let me check you for broken bones,' he said softly, and only when he was satisfied did he help her to her feet.

'Any pain?' Halley asked, as she gave Mary a quick visual scan. A dark patch of liquid on the side of Mary's right calf muscle made Halley crouch down. Sure enough, it was bleeding. Halley couldn't see much through Mary's tights, and in order for her to have a proper look at it they'd need to go somewhere a bit more private.

'I'm fine,' Mary protested, obviously embarrassed by what had happened. The festivities out in the hall had stopped at the crash and soon a few people were coming in to investigate what had happened.

'You've cut your leg, Mary,' Halley said. 'And judging from the amount of blood it's going to require sutures. Is there a first-aid kit around somewhere?' she asked the ladies.

'We'll take her in my car.' Max took Mary's pulse and checked her eyes, tilting her head towards the kitchen light. 'Did you hit your head?'

'No. I…I slipped on…' Mary couldn't finish her sentence and she was starting to shake.

'I need a blanket or a large coat, please,' Halley said to the room in general.

'Mary? Mary?' Bernard came into the kitchen and hurried towards his wife. The shock of seeing her standing amidst a pile of broken plates and pooling blood had him stopping still in his tracks. He edged a little closer, mindful of the mess. 'What happened? Is she all right, Max?'

'I want to take her to hospital, Bernard,' Max said as Halley reached for a clean teatowel and pressed it to Mary's calf. 'Pass me that chair, please.' He pointed to the side of the room. Bernard stood still. 'Bernard, get me that chair, please,' he said more forcefully.

'Oh, *me*?' Bernard quickly got the chair. 'Sorry. I thought you were talking to one of the workers. Why does she need a chair?'

'We need to elevate her leg and get a dressing on that cut. Once we've had a good look at it, we'll take her to hospital.'

'*Hospital?* How long will that take? I have a speech to make.' He pointed in the direction of the hall full of people.

'G-go,' Mary said to her husband through her chattering teeth.

Halley sensed that Mary wanted him gone. 'Mary will be fine,' she reassured him. 'Once the dinner is over, you can stop by the hospital to see how she is.'

Bernard looked at Halley before turning his gaze to Max. 'Halley's right,' Max said with a nod. As soon as he heard it from Max, Bernard left the kitchen, returning to the hall to give a report and allay any fears.

Within seconds Sheena Albright came in, offering her help. They sat Mary down and Halley started riffling through the first-aid kit someone had handed her. After they'd both examined the cut, Halley pressed a bandage to it, trying to absorb the blood so they could at least transfer her to the hospital without leaving a trail. Sheena attended to the small cuts and abrasions on Mary's hands and arms but the most they needed were plasters.

When they were ready, Max brought his car to the rear doors and together they carried Mary out to his car. Halley sat in the back with Mary's head resting on her knee and her legs elevated.

'How are you doing?' she asked softly.

'Feeling a little bit faint,' Mary whispered, her eyes closed.

'We're almost there. You're going to be all right,' Halley reassured her.

Within minutes Max was pulling into the hospital car park, Sheena having called ahead to notify the staff of their imminent arrival. 'I need BP, neurovascular obs and get the local anaesthetic ready,' Max ordered as they wheeled Mary down towards the treatment room. After they'd put on protective clothing and medical gloves, Sheena helped Halley to drape and clean the wound site.

'Definitely requires sutures,' she said softly to Max. 'How's Mary holding up?'

'She's doing fine.'

'Good. All right, I'll just give her a local and we'll get it organised.'

Max explained what they were going to do and Halley waited until Mary had signed the consent form before she sutured the wound closed.

'A mighty neat job, Dr Ryan,' Max observed with a smile, and Halley was elated by his praise. She returned his smile, accepting the moment for the precious gift it was. Soon, when her work here was done and she returned to Melbourne, Halley would be able to look back on moments like these and sigh with longing and loss.

'How are you feeling, Mary?' she asked as she came around to look at her patient.

Sheena started clearing things away and left them alone to talk.

'OK.'

Halley brushed a piece of hair out of Mary's eyes. 'You'll be up and baking in no time.' Her words brought a smile to Mary's lips. 'Bernard should be here soon, and then he can take you home.'

'No!' The smile disappeared instantly and Mary tried to sit up.

'Whoa,' Halley said, glancing over at Max, who was as surprised as herself with Mary's reaction.

'Don't make me go home, Halley. *Please!* Keep me in…overnight.' Mary reached out and grabbed hold of Halley's hand, her gaze pleading.

'Uh…' Halley glanced over at Max again, who quickly nodded. 'Uh…sure, Mary. Of course you can stay here. We should really observe you for at least twenty-four hours. It was wrong of me to assume you could manage at home. Of course you need to rest for a while.'

'Halley's right. We don't want you accidentally tearing out those stitches,' Max added. 'Do you want to see Bernard when he comes in?'

'I…I'm a bit tired.'

'Fair enough. Try to get some sleep. I'll get Sheena to organise a bed for you.'

'Thank you,' Mary whispered as she closed her eyes. They left her to rest. Halley opened her mouth to say something but Max placed a finger across his lips. He spoke to the nurse, giving his instructions, before walking into a small kitchenette and closing the door behind them.

'I can't believe it,' he said, shaking his head slightly as he walked over to the urn and made two cups of coffee, just adding milk to both. 'I know you told me this morning about your visit to Mary yesterday, but…' He shook his head again. 'I can't believe Mary doesn't want to see her husband.'

Halley accepted the coffee with thanks. 'This morning seems a lifetime ago.' She sighed. This morning she hadn't realised she was in love with this man, and now that she knew it was tearing her apart. She pushed all thoughts of her relationship with Max, or lack thereof, to the back of her mind and focused on their patient. 'Now that Mary's actually admitted to there being a problem, she doesn't want things to go back to the way they were. It's not that she doesn't care for Bernard. I believe it's quite the opposite. It's just that there's not a lot of…communication going on between them.'

'She's been coming to see me for weeks,' Max said, starting to pace the room, 'with trifling ailments that really didn't need any attention at all. I knew she was anxious about something but I could never quite get her to trust me enough, yet you've accomplished so much more in just six days!'

'It's only gender, Max. Your skills as a doctor have nothing to do with this situation. It's because I'm female that Mary opened up to me.' There was a knock on the door and Max called for the person to enter.

'Sorry to interrupt,' Sheena said. 'Bernard's here and demanding to see his wife.'

'Right. Thanks, Sheena. Is Mary's bed ready?'

'Yes.'

'Good. Get her organised, please. Show Bernard through here, thanks.' When the sister had gone, he said softly, 'Let me do all the talking.'

'Sure.' Halley took a sip of her coffee. When Bernard

was shown in, Max offered him tea or coffee, which he declined, asking to see his wife.

'I'll take you to her in a minute, Bernard. Have a seat and I'll tell you what we've done.' Max explained the procedure and gave the prognosis for the recovery of Mary's leg. 'She'll need to stay off it for a few days. No cooking, no cleaning, no housework. Complete bed rest.'

'But I've got meetings and work to get done.'

Halley clenched her jaw tight, remembering that she'd agreed to let Max handle him.

'OK. I'll have someone organise house-cleaning and meals to be cooked. Mary's done it for so many other people in the community, I'm sure there'll be plenty of people willing to help out.'

'Or I could ask my mother to come down for a few days.'

Halley's eyes widened in alarm. From what Mary had told her, Bernard's parents were part of the problem. She shook her head slightly and Max nodded slowly.

'Probably not worth it, Bernard. As I said, it would only be for a few days, and I'm sure the community would be only too happy to help out. For the moment, though, Mary's sleeping. The cut was quite deep so we've given her something for the pain, and that's what's made her so drowsy. Rest is going to do her the world of good and she'll be up and around in no time.' Max drained his cup and headed for the door. 'So let's go see her.'

'Ah…wait.' Bernard stood and fished his car keys out of his jacket pocket. 'Perhaps it's best if we don't disturb her. After all, the sooner she can rest, the sooner she'll be up and about again, right?'

'Exactly,' Max replied. 'Shall I walk you out?'

'No. I'm fine.' The two men shook hands. Bernard didn't even bother to acknowledge Halley's presence before leaving the room.

'Are you all right?' Max asked, as though he was trying to gauge her reaction.

'Fine.' She gritted her teeth before smiling. 'I'm used to it.'

'What? People being rude to you?'

Halley shrugged. 'When you come to a town with the possibility of closing down a hospital, well, yeah.'

'But his attitude had nothing to do with that tonight.'

'No. His attitude is because I've spoken to his wife about their problems. As far as Bernard is concerned, his dirty laundry is being aired in public. When Mary told me that she'd spoken to Bernard about tracking her cycle, he told her that he wasn't concerned with it and that the only way to conceive a child was to have regular intercourse. I've interfered in the most private aspect of his life so, of course, he resents me. The fact that I'm female, a qualified medical practitioner and am here to possibly recommend the hospital be closed are just bonuses.'

Max smiled. 'I admire your optimism.'

'Why, thank you.' Halley took her cup to the sink and rinsed it. She smothered a yawn. 'Excuse me. I think the day is definitely catching up with me.'

'Let's go check on our two patients and get out of here.'

'Sounds like a good plan.'

Mary was sleeping soundly so they left her in peace. Alan Kempsey was talking animatedly with Agnes, who'd just returned from the Christmas dinner.

'How's young Mary?' Agnes asked.

'She'll be fine,' Max answered.

'That's good to hear,' Alan said. He looked at them thoughtfully before saying, 'I can't say I know Mary Simpson all that well. We all know Bernard, of course, but Mary…' He shook his head. 'I can tell she's a nice woman.'

'She is,' Halley said, 'and right now, Alan,' she said,

hoping to steer the conversation away from Mary, 'if you have a good night's sleep, we might actually let you go home in the morning.'

'And about time, too,' he said.

Halley picked up the chart from the end of his bed and read his observation record. 'Looking very good,' she commented, and handed it to Max.

'Yes,' Alan said, his eyebrows wiggling up and down, 'but I've known that for years.'

Halley groaned and rolled her eyes, but smiled anyway. 'Very funny.' She sneaked a glance at Max, not wanting him to think she was flirting again. There was a scowl on his face but his gaze was riveted on the chart in front of him.

'As Halley said, it looks good. You'll still experience the dizziness, but it's probably the same as the last time you hit your head. We'll be around in the morning to check on you and will make the decision then,' he said briskly.

'I guess that's the best I can hope for,' Alan murmured, but waved good-naturedly as they left.

Halley waited until they'd said goodnight to the nursing staff and were walking to his car before she spoke. 'Are you happy with Alan's situation? Do you think he'll be able to cope at home by himself?'

He stopped by her door and opened it. Halley frowned. He'd never opened her door before. She climbed in and did up her seat belt, watching Max as he strode around the front of the car before opening his own door.

'He should be fine. As before, Agnes will bring him a meal every day, and with Kylie and myself visiting him regularly there should be no other complications.'

'Unless he has another fall,' Halley remarked.

Max shook his head. 'I sincerely hope he doesn't.'

'Perhaps Kylie could give him some lessons on how to cope better with his crutches.'

'I'll speak to her about it.' Max started the engine and pulled out onto the road.

'Right.' They were silent for a few long minutes. Halley started to feel uneasy in the confined, intimate space of the car. Say something—anything, she told herself, and as the only neutral topic she could think of was their patients, she said, 'Hopefully Mary will be feeling better in the morning.'

'Agreed.' Max shook his head. 'Why didn't Mary want to go home?'

'I don't know but I'm sure we'll soon find out. I'd already planned to do some medical tests about why it's painful when she has sex, so I may as well get it under way tomorrow morning.'

'What do you think might be wrong?'

Halley shrugged. 'There are quite a few possibilities and we just have to rule them out one by one. It might be a simple infection that can be cleared up with medication.' She shrugged again. 'We won't know until we get some tests organised.'

'Good.'

'I often wonder how people get together, what attracted them to each other,' she mused out loud after a few more moments of silence. 'My parents, for example, had a love of horses. They'd always wanted a little property in the country where they could relax and ride.'

'And did they do it?'

'Yes. Only since Dad retired, but I've never seen them both so happy.'

'He doesn't have a lot to do with the business, then?'

'Oh, sure, but they just drive down for a couple of days, do what they have to do and then head back to the place

that makes them happy.' Halley sighed. 'When she's baking and making things are the only times Mary seems to
be happy. What's Bernard like?'

'Chauvinistic,' Max replied.

'I picked up that much. Anything else?'

'What do you mean?'

'Well, have you seen the two of them together at all? Do
they have a group they belong to? An activity they both
like doing?'

He frowned. 'Not that I know of. Generally, when I've
seen them, they've always been apart. Doing their own
thing.'

Halley sighed longingly. 'I think I could only ever settle
for a marriage like my parents'. They have love and sharing.' She spoke softly as she gazed out of the window into
the dark night. 'They're committed to each other and support each other in everything. They're soul-mates.'

'Not everybody views marriage the same as you do.'
Max pulled into his driveway and garaged the car. He cut
the engine and climbed out without saying another word.
Halley scrambled from the car, following Max as he headed
for his front door.

'That's true,' she replied, 'but personally, Max, I can't
understand how people just drift into marriage and expect
it to work.'

Max stopped and faced her. 'Are you referring to
Christina and myself?'

'No, Max. We were having a discussion.'

'No, Halley. You were listing your prerequisites for marriage. They may be your views but not everyone in the
world holds firm to them. Christina and I have a good and
trusting relationship.'

'I have no doubt that you do,' she returned forcefully.
'As I said, I wasn't talking about you. I was making ob-

servations based on my parents' marriage. It's my yardstick and I'm happy it's a positive one.'

'So I suppose that means *my* yardstick isn't positive? My father *loved* my mother—and she left him. He was *never* the same.' Max glared at her before sadly shaking his head.

'Max,' Halley said softly, her gaze imploring. 'This situation with Mary and Bernard has obviously disturbed you.'

'What do you *really* know about it? You've seen Mary, what, twice? And you only met Bernard tonight. I've known them since they moved here and they're *my* patients, not yours. I'm the one who lives here permanently. I'm the one who'll be seeing them through whatever it is they need seeing through. Not you. You'll be gone at the end of next week, Halley and perhaps *then* my life can return to normal.' He looked down into her face, his eyes as cold as ice. 'You'll be gone and that's all there is to it.'

CHAPTER NINE

MAX slammed his front door shut and walked through to the kitchen. He glanced back at the door. The last time he'd slammed a door had been when his mother had left. He shook his head and switched the kettle on before slumping down onto a chair at the table.

Halley Ryan. She'd caused him all sorts of grief this past week and he couldn't wait until she left. She was just like his mother. She was flighty and spontaneous. He was all about neatness and order whilst Halley was the complete opposite.

He freely admitted to a physical attraction, but there was nothing more. Of one thing Max was certain. He *refused* to follow in his father's footsteps and fall for a woman who would no doubt leave him when she received a better offer. Hadn't Halley been travelling for the past two years? She would *never* want to settle down in one place—especially in a country town such as Heartfield.

Then again, she was showing every sign of enjoying her time here. She appeared to like the country, and her love of rock-climbing showed she was an outdoors type of person. Also, during her time overseas she'd mainly been based in country areas. She was a good doctor, which showed commitment and strength.

And when Max had pressed his lips against hers—so fleetingly—he'd felt as though he'd come home.

Max groaned and stood up, disgusted with himself for feeling this way about her. He was a grown man. Surely he could control his emotions. Deciding to forget the tea, he stalked to the bathroom and got ready for bed. It wasn't until he was lying beneath the warm blankets that he heard the muted sounds coming from next door.

A man laughed and he remembered that her brothers were still in town. He'd been surprised to find he liked them. They ran a multi-million-dollar business and were still very down to earth. He smiled wryly, remembering the way Dan had looked at them. Dan was definitely impressed with wealthy people, and the shock he'd openly displayed at discovering Halley to be their sister had been…priceless. Max didn't have a lot of time for people as false as Dan. It was a pity Christina had to have such a disagreeable father but it couldn't be helped.

Christina! Max sat up and looked at the clock. It was after midnight and only now did he remember that he hadn't said goodnight to Christina. He'd simply rushed out to the hospital without a backward glance. He was sure she'd understand but, still, it was bad manners on his part.

'Damn Halley,' he muttered. She so filled his thoughts it made him forget everything else!

The following morning, Halley was up and dressed before the sun rose. She took a cup of coffee out to the front verandah and sipped at it while she watched the first golden rays spread over the town. It was a beautiful sight and she sighed, amazed to find a sense of calm filling her turbulent thoughts.

She'd hardly slept a wink last night, thinking about the man next door. She was deeply distressed that Max could think she'd intentionally cause him pain by speaking as she had. She hadn't! She'd only been saying what *she* thought important in a marriage.

This, coupled with the fact that he couldn't wait until she left, had given her such an awful night that she wasn't surprised at seeing the dark circles beneath her eyes. Yesterday had been a hectic day, and emotionally it had completely drained Halley of all her reserves.

She loved Max…and there was nothing she could do about it. She could *never* settle for second best so it appeared she was doomed to a life of solitude. Right at the moment she was looking forward to getting through this next week with as little social contact with Max as possible. Professionally, they worked perfectly together, but anything else…

Halley shook her head and sighed again. A door closed behind her and she turned, thinking it might be one of her brothers.

'Good morning.' Max nodded politely. He was dressed for work, just as she was, even though it was Sunday. They stared at each other for a long moment before Max shifted his briefcase to his other hand and slowly walked in her direction. He gazed out at the spectacular scene before them.

'Majestic, isn't it?'

'Yes,' she replied. Halley's heart was pounding furiously against her ribs and she took a deep breath to try and steady her mounting nerves. 'Max?' she said eventually.

'Hmm?'

'I'm…sorry if I…said anything to hurt you last night. It *wasn't* intentional.'

He nodded slightly. 'It's fine.'

'Really? You're not just saying that to be polite?'

Max smiled slightly. 'No, Halley.'

Halley brightened and acknowledged that a few minutes in his presence was all it took to get her back in a good mood. She drained her cup and checked her watch. 'Almost half past seven. We'd better get to the hospital. That way we can do a ward round and get to church on time. I wanted to go and thank the ladies who did all the preparation for last night's big event.'

Max nodded, turned and walked to his car. Halley watched him go, admiring the length of his body, his long legs and the broad shoulders that appeared to be carrying the weight of the world.

She sighed with longing before realising that if she didn't make a move there was no way she'd accomplish anything. She returned her cup to the kitchen, checked that her brothers were still snoring away in the room that had previously been her bedroom before heading out to the car.

It seemed silly to take two cars, but who knew where Max had to go after the hospital? He hadn't said anything to her but for the moment she felt that separate cars meant separate lives, and that was the way they should keep it.

'He's engaged to Christina and you're leaving at the end of the week,' she told herself firmly as she drove. Despite those facts, Halley couldn't help the joy and elation she felt when she was with him. He made her happy. What was wrong with that? She might be in love with him but she also knew the score. Max was a man of principles and she wouldn't have him any other way. He'd given his word to Christina and he was going to keep it.

'Even though it's wrong,' she told herself bleakly as she parked next to his car. As she climbed from the car, briefcase in hand, she squared her shoulders and put her professionalism in place.

Max was already on the ward, standing at the base of Alan Kempsey's bed, reading his chart. Sheena was plumping up Alan's pillows and straightening his bedcovers.

Alan smiled brightly. 'Good morning, Halley.'

Max handed her the chart without a word and she read the nursing report from the previous night. 'I've given him a check-up and everything is fine,' Max mumbled.

'Good news.' She nodded encouragingly. 'So you're back to daily house calls.'

'Yes,' Alan said, and looked from her to Max. Halley had a strange feeling that Alan wanted to say something but was still working up the courage. Sheena was called out to the phone and everyone was silent as she left. Alan cleared his throat and looked down at his hands.

'Let me go over your last lot of X-ray results one last time,' Max said, leaving the two of them alone. Halley stayed at the base of the bed and returned the chart to its holder.

'Um…Halley…' Alan's gaze strayed to the open doorway before it returned to her. 'While Max is out of the room, I wanted to ask you something.'

Halley's apprehension grew. 'Sure.'

'Well…I was…um…wondering whether…you might come and do the house calls this week? Uh…you know…so we can talk more about rock-climbing before you go,' he added as an afterthought.

'I see,' she said slowly and took a deep breath. 'Actually, Alan…' She held his gaze. 'It's much better for your long-term management if Max continues to do your house calls. He's been your GP from the start so it's best to keep it that way. Within another week I'll be gone.'

Alan looked down at his hands before meeting her gaze once more. 'Uh…sure. I can see the logic in that, but why don't you stay?'

'Stay?'

'Yeah. Stay here in Heartfield. I'm sure we could use another doctor and, well, you seem to like it here.'

Halley was stunned. She'd never thought of staying but knew immediately what the answer was. 'I can't,' she told him earnestly. 'I have…things to do when I finish here. The Victorian Department for Health will most likely have another assignment for me as soon as I've finished this one.'

'But you wouldn't have to take it, would you?' Alan persisted.

Halley shrugged, feeling like a caged animal. How could she stay here? She *couldn't*, because she was in love with a man who was already engaged to someone else. To see Max and Christina married, to work with him day in, day out and not be able to *be* with him, would be…a death sentence.

'It wouldn't work, Alan,' she said finally. 'Max is your doctor. It's best to keep it that way.' She forced a smile. 'At least you get your release from this place today. That's something positive to focus on.' As she finished talking, Max came back into the room, along with Agnes.

'Good morning, all,' Agnes said, her features bright and cheerful. It was a complete contrast to the first time Halley had met her on the night Alan had had his fall. It was good to know that her brother meant a lot to her. Despite the ups and downs, they still cared for each other and that was evident in Agnes's expression.

This was the reason Halley loved being a doctor. Helping people. Seeing them on the way to recovery. Although Alan still had a long way to go, he had family supporting him. From that alone, Halley knew that he'd eventually make it through this ordeal.

'X-rays are looking fine,' Max announced with a bright smile. Halley frowned. What was he up to?

'At least promise to sign my cast before you go,' Alan said, as he again looked from Halley to Max.

'Promise.' She breathed a mental sigh of relief. 'Next patient, Dr Pearson?' she asked, and at his nod they said goodbye to Alan and Agnes. Sheena was still on the phone so they proceeded to Mary's room, which was across the hall.

'Nicely handled,' Max said softly.

Halley was surprised at his comment and stopped at the door to Mary's room. 'Pardon?'

'Alan. I heard what you said to him, Halley, and you handled it very well indeed.'

'What, no lectures about leading him on?'

'No.' Max shook his head slightly. Their gazes held and Halley felt that same old spiralling sensation building deep within her at his presence. She leaned against the door for support but only succeeded in pushing it open with her shoulder.

She stumbled into the room, startling Mary but making her patient smile at the same time. 'Sorry,' Halley mumbled. 'How are you feeling this morning?'

'Better, thank you,' Mary replied meekly. Halley and Max read her chart, both noticing that Mary did look better than when they'd left last night.

'Let's take a peek at your leg.' Halley lifted the pristine bedcovers. 'I'm really proud of that,' she told them both. 'That's a fine stitching job, even if I do say so myself.'

'Don't tell me you can't sew either?' Max remarked drolly, but the smile on his lips belied the severity of his words.

'As you can see, I'm not too bad with a needle,' she admitted. 'But knitting—forget it!'

Mary laughed and then winced. 'Ooh.'

Halley and Max were instantly alert. 'What's wrong? Pain somewhere?'

'I just ache all over,' she groaned.

'You will do,' Max said. 'You came down mighty hard. It's a wonder you didn't fracture your hip.'

Mary looked at them both, her eyes wide and frightened. 'What's going to happen next?'

'Well,' Halley said, 'remember on Friday that I wanted to talk about some tests?' She waited for Mary's nod. 'Good. Max and I feel it's better if we get the ball rolling sooner rather than later.'

'Oh… OK. What sort of tests?'

'I need a blood sample and a urine sample. We need to rule out any infections you might have.'

'*Infections!* I thought people who had…lots of…partners got infections. I've only ever, well, been with Bernard.'

'There are different types of infections,' Max said softly. 'You may have a bladder infection or a kidney infection and these can be cleared up with a course of antibiotics.'

'B-but the pain's been there for years. Ever since…we…' Mary looked down at her clenched hands.

'Since the first time you had sex?' Halley asked, and Mary nodded.

'Mary, forgive me,' Max said, and Halley held her breath. 'Does Bernard *force* you to have intercourse?'

'No. Oh, no,' Mary reassured them quickly. 'If I say no, then he doesn't…*force* me. Bernard is *much* too much of a gentleman to do that. It's just that whenever we do…well…you know, it…hurts. I've told Bernard but he said that doing it more often will help the pain. I thought at first that it was normal to feel pain but now I'm not so sure. That's why I…' She looked down at her hands again. 'That's why I came to…' She glanced quickly at Max.

'That's why you started coming to see me,' he finished, and she nodded.

'I didn't know how to say it.' Mary's words were barely audible and Halley could tell she was highly embarrassed.

'That's all over now,' Halley said reassuringly. 'And I

want you to know that you're not alone in feeling this way, Mary.'

'That's true,' Max added. 'A lot of women experience pain during intercourse, and nine times out of ten there is a reason for that pain.'

'This is what we need to find out, and there's no time like the present.' Halley ordered a complete blood work-up and urine analysis, hoping to rule out any diseases.

'Dr Ryan?' Mary called softly just after Max had walked out the door. 'Have you got a spare moment?'

'Uh…sure.' Halley glanced at Max, who was out of Mary's sight. 'Give us a second?' she whispered, and he nodded. Halley came back into the room. 'What's on your mind?' she asked gently with a smile.

'You know how I asked you if you'd ever been in love, and you said it was as infectious as laughter, as consuming as a sneeze and sometimes as annoying as the hiccups?'

'Yes.' Halley now agreed with that statement more than when she'd initially made it. Right now it felt as though she constantly had the hiccups.

'Well, I think you were right. I thought I was in love with Bernard when he asked me to marry him. I had stars in my eyes. But now…well, living with someone can really open your eyes and help you to see the *real* person.'

'Hmm?'

Mary's bottom lip quivered. 'I do love him…but it's not the way…you know…it used to be in the beginning. Is that wrong?'

'No,' Halley said instantly. 'It's not wrong. It happens sometimes. My mother also said that any relationship requires open and honest communication, but most of all it must be constant. Marriages can have their ups and downs but remember it's the down times that make you appreciate the up times.'

Mary nodded. 'I know it seems that Bernard cares more about his work than me, but really he's quite attentive and very sweet at times, although he doesn't seem to have a clue what's going on. How do I make him understand?'

'Perhaps what's happening to you now *will* make him understand. You begged us to keep you in here last night. What was your main reason for doing that?'

Mary shrugged. 'I guess I was feeling a little uncertain. Would Bernard look after me? Would he *want* to look after me? He's never told me that he loves me…' Mary choked on a sob and Halley quickly reached for a tissue. 'And I don't know what to do any more.' Tears were flowing down her face as she quietly cried the hurt out. Halley placed her arm around the woman's shoulders and murmured soothing words. 'I just couldn't face the anxiety last night,' Mary hiccuped as a fresh bout of tears erupted.

Halley heard the door open and Max peered around it. He raised his eyebrows questioningly but Halley shook her head. He nodded and left them alone. Communication, she thought. As Mary continued to cry and talk about her life with Bernard, Halley realised that there was no way she'd make it to church this morning. At least she could help this woman to vent her emotions, which had obviously been building up for quite some time.

Some time later, as Mary slept peacefully, Halley went in search of Max. Sheena had told her that he'd returned to his office to catch up on some paperwork while he waited for her. She knocked on his open door and he instantly looked up.

'How is she?'

'Sleeping,' Halley answered as she slumped down into a chair opposite him. 'So, how many trained marriage counsellors do you have in this town?' she asked dryly, already knowing the answer.

'Things that bad?'

'We need to get Bernard to talk to his wife. We need to get Mary to talk to her husband. We need a round-table discussion and the sooner, the better.'

'Bernard won't appreciate outside interference.'

'I gathered as much, but Mary needs it. *Trained* interference,' Halley added. 'Not a family member or a friend from town. They need to start communicating, and fast. The first thing Bernard needs to understand is that this pain Mary feels *isn't* her fault. It *isn't* the reason why they haven't conceived. He doesn't force her to have sex, but I suspect his attitude is the main reason Mary believes her *pain* is why they have no children.' Halley stood and started to pace around the room.

Max sat back in his chair and watched her. 'You have steam coming out of your ears,' he joked.

'I'm not surprised after listening to what Mary's had to say. I think she's just unloaded a lifetime of pent-up emotions and, although I've done basic psychology, I'm not a trained psychologist! I feel angry and frustrated with both Bernard *and* Mary's parents. From the sound of it, her father practically talked her into being in love with Bernard, pointing out the way he paid her attention—that sort of thing—so that when Bernard proposed Mary fancied herself in love with him.'

'Aren't you letting your personal feelings get in the way?' Max asked.

'Hey, *mate*, she vented on me and now I'm venting on you. Yes, I'm getting personal, and I know I shouldn't be, which is why I think *both of us* should counsel them.'

'Halley, you're only here for another five days!'

'That's all the more reason to get the ball rolling. Mary's finally unloaded herself; she's opened up. She's found the courage to tell us what's been bothering her. Sure, it took her a while but she's done it. It's a cry for help. She's taken the step, Max, and she won't allow herself to go backwards. For the first time in her life she's standing up for herself, and if Bernard doesn't face the fact that something needs to change, he may not have a wife for much longer.'

'She's not suicidal?' Max asked quickly.

'No. She's just saying *enough*! She's saying she doesn't want to be treated like this any more. It's not that she doesn't enjoy what she does, and by that I mean being a housewife and joining committees and cooking and all that, but what she does want is some respect from her husband. Respect as a person, an individual, as well as a partner in their marriage. Is that too much for her to ask?'

Max exhaled slowly and shook his head. 'No. No. I'll speak to Bernard when he comes and set up a meeting for tonight.'

'Good.'

'To start with you'd better give me some of the preliminary details Mary's discussed with you so we can plan a strategy for the counselling sessions.'

Halley nodded. 'Sure. First, though, I'll get us some coffee.'

'Good idea.'

Almost two hours later the phone on Max's desk shrilled to life, startling them both. 'It might be Sheena saying that Bernard is here,' Halley suggested hopefully. So far Bernard hadn't come to see his wife, but, then, as Max had reasoned, church didn't usually finish until just before midday.

'It's an outside line,' he told her. 'Dr Pearson,' he said into the receiver. 'Hello, Christina.' He listened. 'Yes, she's here, too.' Max glanced at his watch and then at the clock on the wall. 'All right. How about we meet at the bakery and have lunch? See you soon.' He replaced the receiver.

'Half past twelve. No wonder I'm hungry.' He stood and stretched his arms above his head and Halley drank in the movement of his shirt pulling tight around his flexed arm muscles, his trousers dipping slightly as he stretched first to one side, then the other.

Her pulse rate increased and so did her breathing. His stretching action should be declared illegal, she thought. When he'd finished, his gaze met hers. Halley quickly lowered her head and cleared her throat. She hoped he hadn't seen her looking at him because she was positive the expression on her face had said she'd rather eat *him* for lunch than any food.

She glanced surreptitiously at him to find him looking down at her, a small knowing smile creasing his face. Halley clenched her jaw and on impulse decided that fair was fair. She, too, stood and stretched, mimicking his action, enjoying the way her muscles loosened up slightly.

When she'd finished, she raised her eyes to meet his and was satisfied to see him pulling at his shirt collar with his index finger. 'Shall we go?' she asked sweetly. Not waiting for an answer, she turned and headed towards the door. She stopped suddenly and turned to face him. 'Oh, what about Bernard?'

Max shrugged. 'We'll catch up with him later. Let's go eat. We'll take my car.' After they'd told Sheena where they were going, they headed out to the car park. They continued to talk about their strategy for Mary and Bernard on the drive. When they arrived at the bakery, Halley realised they weren't only meeting Christina but her brothers as well.

'Hi,' she said, giving them both a hug. 'All packed?'

Jon laughed and slung his arm about Halley. 'Anyone would think she was trying to get rid of us.' He directed his comments directly to Christina, who smiled back at him.

Oh, yes, Halley wanted them gone, especially as it appeared Jon and Christina had hit it off.

'So what have you boys been doing this morning?' she asked after they'd ordered and sat down.

'We've been talking with Dan,' Jon replied. 'We're looking to expand the manufacturing division, and as it won't be a retail outlet we can base it anywhere.'

Halley stared at Jon in amazement. 'And you want to base it *here*? In *Heartfield*?'

'Why not?' Jon spread his arms wide. 'It's not that far from Melbourne and the scenery is…beautiful.'

Halley looked at Marty and he shrugged. 'Sorry, Squirt. This is Jon's project.'

'I'll just bet it is,' Halley mumbled.

Their food was brought to the table, and while the boys and Christina were chatting Max leaned over and said quietly, 'Why do you think it's a bad idea for your brothers to open a plant here?'

Halley looked at him, dumbfounded. Was he completely blind? Couldn't he see that Jon was interested in his own fiancée? 'So you don't mind?'

'No. I think it's a great idea. It would be good for this community to have a new project to embrace.'

Halley simply shook her head.

'What?' Max asked, but his attention was drawn by Marty before Halley could reply.

'So how did your father react to the news?' Halley asked Christina, guessing how Dan felt but wanting to hear it just the same.

'He's ecstatic. He and Bernard went back to their office to discuss it in more detail,' Christina replied, her body bubbling with excitement as she gazed happily at Jon. 'It's such a wonderful idea and would be just perfect for our community.'

At least that explained why Bernard hadn't come to visit his wife! They ate lunch, with the new Planet Electronics scheme the main topic of conversation. Afterwards, Halley gave both of her brothers a hug and kiss. As she wrapped her arms about Jon's neck, she whispered, 'Oh, and thanks for contacting Marla.'

'No problem,' he whispered back.

'Drive carefully,' she told them both. 'And call me when you get in so I know you've arrived safely.'

'She's worse than our mother,' Marty said in a conspiratorial whisper. Everyone laughed and Halley waved as she climbed back into Max's car.

'I like your brothers,' he said as they headed back to the hospital. 'I'm glad we met.' Halley murmured a noncommittal reply. 'You really don't like the idea of them opening a plant here, do you?'

'No, Max.'

'Why? Give me one good reason.'

Halley wasn't sure what to say. Should she tell him that Jon had fallen for Christina? Did Max feel so secure in the relationship he had with his fiancée that he didn't mind her having close relationships with other men? Halley chewed on her bottom lip. How could he not have noticed what was going on? Then again, she'd only noticed it because she knew her brother far too well. Yet he *was* her brother, and if she said anything it might show him in a bad light.

Halley was confused. Where did her loyalties lie? With her brother or the man she loved?

Max pulled the car into the hospital car park and switched off the engine. He turned slightly to face her. 'Come on. Give. What's your reason? Why do you think it's such a bad idea?'

Halley undid her seat belt and looked at him. 'I don't think it's a bad *business* idea. I mean, the land and housing here would be cheaper than in an outer suburb of Melbourne, so those costs would be decreased. I agree that the area is lovely and the community would certainly embrace such a project.'

'Hmm…go on.'

Halley took a deep breath. 'It's just that…well…it would mean that the boys—especially Jon, as this is apparently his project—would be spending more time here.'

'Climbing, you mean?'

'Oh, that too, but, no, that wasn't what I meant.' Halley looked down at her hands, praying for her beeper to sound or his phone to ring or an emergency to happen—*anything* that might get her off the hook. Nothing happened.

'Are you referring to the fact that your brother appears…interested in my fiancée?'

CHAPTER TEN

THE look of complete astonishment on Halley's face was one he'd remember for ever. Max thankfully rested his head against the pillows, glad to be finally home. The day had been full of surprises, some good, some…not so good.

On the positive side, Bernard had shown genuine concern over Mary's health, and even though he'd initially refused to talk about their relationship they'd eventually worn him down. Mary had asked him to go to counselling with her or their marriage would continue to struggle. He'd seemed genuinely surprised to find that she wasn't very happy.

On the other hand, his thoughts kept turning to Halley and Christina. He hadn't been surprised to see Christina a little more animated than usual. Since yesterday morning, when Halley's brother had first met her, he'd been aware of a subtle change in his fiancée. At lunch, however, he'd come to realise that Christina appeared to be as interested in Jon as Jon was in her.

What *had* surprised him, though, was that he hadn't felt even the slightest twinge of jealousy. Even now, as he thought about the way Christina had smiled at Jon, the way she'd laughed at his jokes—nothing!

Yet the first time Alan Kempsey had grinned at Halley, Max had felt the sudden urge to tear the other man to shreds. Jealousy in all its glory!

The thought made his head ache more and he switched off the light and closed his eyes.

He didn't want to think about it any more. He just

wanted to rest his body and mind by having a good sleep. He turned his thoughts towards music, as thinking about a classical piece often helped him to fall asleep. Employing relaxation techniques and controlling his breathing, Max started to unwind.

Moments later, a faint humming noise came through the wall from next door. Halley! Just when he thought he'd banished her to the back of his mind, something always happened to bring her back to the fore. Max unclenched his jaw and tried the relaxation techniques again. They didn't work.

He buried his head beneath the pillow as visions of her getting ready for bed entered his mind. She was probably wearing one of those short transparent nighties women were so fond of. No. Halley didn't wear dresses. Boxer shorts and top. Yes. That was more like her. Still, the image almost made him hyperventilate. Her legs would be bare except where the satin boxers started at the top of her thighs. The top would be loose around the arms, clinging subtly to her curves. With one sensual slide of his hand, the satin would ride up, revealing—

Max sat bolt upright in bed, throwing the pillow against the wall as he realised where his thoughts had led him. 'Get out of my head,' he whispered harshly, raking a not-so-steady hand through his hair. The humming stopped and remorse instantly engulfed him. He shouldn't have thrown the pillow. The muffled thud might have startled her.

He should go next door and see if she was all right. Max tossed off the bedcovers and was in the process of standing before he rejected the idea. To go next door now would be to break every vow, every promise he'd made, not only to Christina but to himself as well.

He was attracted to Halley, and even though it was starting to become like a fever that wouldn't break he knew the end was drawing near. He only had to hold on for another six days. Five more working days and then next Saturday Halley would be leaving. For good!

Max collected the pillow before climbing back into bed, straining to hear some noise from next door but not hearing a thing. It sounded as though Halley had gone to bed—her bed that she'd felt compelled to move into the front room. If only he'd met her before he'd proposed to Christina, he thought. Then again, it probably wouldn't have mattered. He and Halley were just too opposite for anything permanent to work between them. Max propped himself up on the pillows, his hands laced behind his head as he stared up at the ceiling. It looked as though sleep was going to be a long time coming tonight.

On Monday and Tuesday Halley forced herself to focus solely on her work. During her daily meetings with Max she remained professional and aloof. He reported that Alan Kempsey was progressing well and coping better with his crutches.

Only her visits to Clarabelle brought her any consolation. With Clarabelle she felt she could be herself, and when she visited her patient on Wednesday it was to see her up and walking about—slowly—the leg ulcer almost completely healed.

'Don't overdo it,' Halley warned.

'That's exactly what Kylie said when she was here,' Clarabelle remarked. 'And I've had Christina in here, fussing, this morning.'

'Christina?' Halley was surprised. It wasn't often that she came in the morning to visit. 'Couldn't she come this afternoon?

'No. She's going with her father to look at the proposed site for that electronics thing your brother is doing.'

Halley's eyes widened in disbelief. 'Is Jon coming to town?'

Clarabelle frowned. 'I don't think so, but for some reason Christina's taking a big interest in this project.' Clarabelle sat down on her bed and swivelled her legs up to rest them. 'That's enough exercise for now. So, tell me…'

'Hmm?' Halley waited.

'More about your brother, Jon. He seems like a nice man.'

Halley's smile was involuntary but she was still a little cautious. 'He is a nice man, and so is my other brother, Marty.'

'I can see why they call him Jupiter. He's quite tall, isn't he?'

'Six feet five. Too tall for me. I like my men about six feet four.'

'Max's height,' Clarabelle said, her gaze boring directly into Halley.

'Is…is *that* how tall Max is? I hadn't noticed.' Halley tried for nonchalance but wasn't sure she succeeded.

'Oh, don't give me that. You insult my intelligence. I know you've noticed *everything* about Max, Halley, and don't try to deny it.'

Halley closed her eyes for a moment, deciding what to do. She liked Clarabelle, they'd formed a connection the instant they'd met, and as she desperately wanted someone to talk to the decision was easy.

'All right, I won't,' she said softly, and opened her eyes. She shrugged. 'I like Max.'

'And…?'

'And what? I'm attracted to him. I like his company—'

'Are you in love with him or not?'

Halley held her breath for a moment before saying quickly, 'Yes.'

'I knew it!' Clarabelle clapped her hands together. 'As soon as you walked into this room last week I could sense the tension between the two of you. Oh, I do so like it when I'm right.'

'So long as you're not going to gloat,' Halley replied.

'Well? What are you going to do?'

'About what?'

'About Max, of course. You can't let him marry Christina. They're almost like…brother and sister, and generally brothers and sisters don't marry.'

'What am I supposed to do? Ask Max to break his word? His commitment to Christina?'

'Yes.'

'Clarabelle! I could *never* do that. One of the things I admire most about Max is that he's honourable. He's trustworthy and giving. To ask him to do that would be to try and change who he is.'

'So you'd rather live the rest of your life alone, knowing that the man you love is married to someone else,' Clarabelle stated. 'Pitiful. I thought you had more backbone than that.'

'Well, obviously I don't.'

'What if Christina were to break off the engagement? Wouldn't that be breaking *her* promise?'

'Forgive me if I offend you, but Christina strikes me as a woman who's been too frightened to put a foot wrong for most of her life.' Clarabelle nodded in agreement. 'If she were to break off her engagement, for whatever reason, it would hopefully be a step towards independence and breaking away from her comfort zones.'

'Double standards.'

'No. Max knew exactly what he was doing when he asked Christina to marry him. For him to break it off would be to go back on his word.'

'So you're saying that Christina didn't know what she was doing when she accepted Max's proposal?'

'Yes.'

'I agree with you. In her father's eyes Max is a respectable man who…cares for Christina and would look after her. My son is a hard man to please and I know Christina likes to please her father. In accepting Max's proposal she has been given a guaranteed safe and comfortable future without stretching her boundaries, without taking a leap of faith and without finding out who she really is.'

Halley nodded. 'To her, Max is safe.'

'Now, with your brother, she's starting to change.' Clarabelle's eyes were bright with excitement. 'Christina came to pick me up and on the drive into town all she could talk about was this giant of a man called Jon, who she found amazing. The last time I saw her that animated was at Christmas when she was eight years old and her father was away. Oh, the three of us girls had a fantastic time that year. I saw the sparks between you and Max during that brief kiss beneath the mistletoe, which is why I can't for the life of me understand what you're waiting for.'

'You're being very presumptuous,' Halley countered. 'Max may be attracted to me but I'm sure he doesn't feel the same way I do. At the moment he can't wait for me to leave. He told me so himself.'

Clarabelle waved her concerns away. 'Codswallop. He's just as much in love with you as you are with him. I'm certain of it. The reason he wants you gone is that you've disrupted his quiet, ordered life far too much for comfort, and the sooner you leave, the sooner he can get his life back on track. Unfortunately, what the dear man hasn't realised yet is that you've changed his life for ever, Halley.'

'Hmm…we'll see.'

Clarabelle laughed. 'You even sound like him. See how

you've unconsciously picked up some of his habits? It's quite cute, really.'

Halley laughed as well and shook her head. 'All I know is that on Saturday morning I drive out of here for good.'

'Oh, I wouldn't count on it,' Clarabelle said, but raised her fingers to her lips when Halley tried to question her further.

Soon it was time for Halley to leave and she headed back down Clarabelle's bumpy track and then towards Mary Simpson's house.

Her leg was healing without complication, which was good, and the tests for infection that Halley had requested had come back with negative results.

'Can you explain to me what it is that I have?' Mary asked as Halley brought in a tray with two cups of tea and some delicious homemade biscuits she'd found in one of Mary's tins.

'Of course. There are many causes for dyspareunia but in your case it's due to spasms of your vaginal muscles. This is a condition we call vaginismus.'

Mary's lower lip began to quiver slightly and Halley smiled encouragingly.

'As I said before, it's not as uncommon as you might think. In your case it's only minor, as most women can't even have a gynaecological examination. A lot of women experience this type of pain and usually it's more psychological than physical.'

Mary nodded. 'You said that before—but...*how*?'

'It may stem from your strict upbringing, coupled with the fact that on your wedding night all you experienced was pain.'

'So you think there's hope for me?'

'Of course there is,' Halley reassured her quickly. 'The fact that Bernard is at least willing to talk about this will make all the difference. The blame for this condition doesn't lie solely with you, Mary. Bernard must learn to help you so that you can both enjoy the experience. It may still take a while but it will happen if you're both committed to making it work.'

'What about children?'

'Physically you're more than capable of conceiving a child but mentally you're just not ready for it. You need to work through this situation first and feel more comfortable with having sex. When I ordered those tests the other day, I also requested some information on your hormone levels and they all checked out quite normally.'

'So that means we can one day have a family.'

Halley nodded. 'One day. The first step is for you and Bernard to feel comfortable talking to each other. You need to understand each other's bodies and not feel inhibited. You'll get through it together, Mary. It just takes persistence and strength and you have both in abundance.'

They talked for a while longer, Halley openly enjoying the delicious biscuits, before she finally said goodbye. 'I'm going to miss you when you leave,' Mary said as Halley put her coat on.

'The feeling is mutual but my contract was only for two weeks.' She shrugged. 'These things happen.'

'You'll come back for a visit, won't you?'

She didn't think so. Instead she forced a smile. 'Anything's possible. See you tomorrow.' With that, she let herself out and walked across the road to where she'd parked her car.

'Oh, Dr Ryan?' she heard, and turned back to Mary's house. No. That wasn't where the call had come from. 'Dr Ryan?' She realised it was coming from Mrs Smythe's house and she headed in that direction.

'Good afternoon, Mrs Smythe,' Halley said as Mrs

Smythe held her front door open. 'Feeling all right today?'
Halley noticed instantly that Mrs Smythe was leaning
heavily on her walking frame. More so than usual.

'Twinges, that's all,' the woman said. 'Me arthritis always plays up in winter.' Halley waited patiently while Mrs
Smythe walked into the kitchen. 'I've made ya some more
casseroles,' she explained.

'Thank you. That's very kind.'

'They're on the bench in reheatable microwave dishes
so it's less fuss for ya,' Mrs Smythe explained as she
rounded the corner into the kitchen. Halley saw three large
dishes on the bench. 'I just need to find a box or something
to put them in so they won't spill in ya car when ya drive
home.'

'What? All of them?'

'Well ya do have three more nights to eat dinner before
ya leave.'

'One would be enough to get me through the next three
nights. The food is so filling.'

'Nonsense.' Mrs Smythe waved a shaky hand in the direction of a door. 'The laundry's through there. Go and see
if ya can find a box to put them in.'

Halley did as she was told and found quite a few boxes
neatly stacked on the top shelf. How on earth had Mrs
Smythe put them up there? Then again, in this community
she probably had someone come round and help her out
once or twice a week. Halley heard a banging sound and
frowned. She pulled the box down and headed back into
the kitchen, just in time to see Mrs Smythe lose her balance,
crying out as she toppled to the floor.

Halley dropped the box and rushed over. She pressed her
fingers to Mrs Smythe's carotid pulse. 'Are you all right?
What happened?'

Mrs Smythe closed her eyes and groaned in pain. Halley

disentangled the walking frame, which was caught between both legs, and moved it out of the way. She pulled her mobile phone off her waistband and quickly called the hospital.

'Sheena, it's Halley. I'm at Mrs Smythe's place and she's sustained a fall.'

'I'll get Max and the ambulance organised immediately,' Sheena replied.

'Don't worry about it,' Mrs Smythe protested after Halley had hung up. Halley was monitoring her closely, checking for broken bones. 'I've had lots of falls and— Oh, ow,' she complained as Halley touched her right leg.

'You've dislocated your hip, Mrs Smythe. That in itself needs hospitalisation. I don't want you to move. I'm just going to get a blanket and pillow to make you a bit more comfortable until Dr Pearson arrives.'

Halley did as she'd said and quickly hurried out to the car for her medical bag. She took Mrs Smythe's blood pressure as well as performing the general round of neurological observations. She also administered analgesic to help control the pain.

'What happened?' Halley asked again while they waited.

'Oh, it was silly of me,' Mrs Smythe grumbled. 'I was only trying to get closer to the bench when me walker got stuck on the corner of the cupboard. I pulled it up too quickly and lost me balance. Silly, silly,' she chastised herself.

'Don't be so hard on yourself. Personally, I think you're just looking to have a holiday in hospital,' Halley teased, and was pleased to see a smile brighten Mrs Smythe's face.

'Oh, get away with ya. Well, at least we still have a hospital for me to go to,' her patient remarked, and Halley felt uncomfortable. 'I know ya've done a good job with ya evaluation,' she said solemnly.

Halley stared down into the old woman's face. This woman who had confronted her on her first day here and who was now so welcoming. Halley had no idea how to tell her she was going to recommend that Heartfield District Hospital be closed.

'Hello?'

'Max,' Halley said softly, and stood. 'In the kitchen,' she called, and rushed out to help him bring the stretcher in. 'She's dislocated her right hip but other than that she's just fine.'

'Her *right* hip?' He waited for Halley's nod. 'Damn.'

'Problem?'

'She had a total hip replacement six months ago.' He crouched down next to Mrs Smythe. 'Looks as though you get a trip to Geelong to see your lovely orthopaedic surgeon again,' he told her.

'Oh, he's a sweet man,' Mrs Smythe said with a smile.

'Let's get you organised,' he said, and they worked together to get their patient to the hospital where Sheena arranged the transfer while Mrs Smythe had a set of X-rays taken.

'She may even need revision,' Max said as he stared at the films. 'Oh, well, can't be helped. Tell me again what happened.'

Halley filled him in on the details.

'So she'd made some casseroles for you?'

'Yes. Three enormous casseroles.'

'She must really like you.'

'Quite a few people do, Max. It's not that uncommon.'

He frowned at her words and she wondered what sort of bee he had in his bonnet this time. 'So you haven't told her,' he said softly so that only the two of them could hear.

'Told her what?' Halley asked, knowing exactly what he

was talking about. A sinking feeling in the pit of her stomach made her previous appetite disappear.

'Halley, don't play coy with me. It really doesn't suit you. You and I both know the only recommendation you can make to the VDH is for the hospital to close. The last lot of figures you showed me point in that direction.'

'It's not up to me to break the news,' Halley said.

'You just don't want to be the bad guy,' he said and his remark wasn't far from the truth. She'd been welcomed by this community—albeit slowly at first—and they'd made her feel very much at home. Halley didn't want that hostility to return.

'No,' she agreed. 'The VDH will do it.'

'They will,' he said, 'via an official letter which *I* will then need to distribute.'

Halley sighed as the bleakness of the situation sank in. The hostility and the piercing looks that she'd experienced on her first day here would return but, short of a miracle occurring, her only course of action was to recommend the hospital be closed.

'Unless you can find another permanent GP,' she added.

'What?'

'If there were two full-time general practitioners employed at this hospital, then it would be worth keeping it open.'

'Ha!' Max laughed with derision. 'I have a hard enough time getting locums to come here for six months. Young doctors aren't interested in working in the country and old doctors are usually just waiting their time out for retirement. Besides, I've been doing all the work around here for years.'

'Not *all* the work, Max. Just in the time I've been here you've needed me to anaesthetise, help out in emergencies and generally lighten your load. No. The hospital needs two full-time doctors, otherwise you'll be working yourself into an early grave.'

'I'm not the problem here, Halley,' he protested, and she instantly agreed with him. 'Why can't I just keep having locums?'

'Because it costs the VDH and therefore the taxpayers too much. I'll be recommending a locum be stationed here for one month, which will hopefully give you time to advertise the position and get someone to fill it.'

'Impossible!' He turned away from her and shook his head.

Sheena cleared her throat and they turned around. 'Helicopter's just landed,' she told them, and Max yanked the films off the viewer and stuffed them back into their packet.

Mrs Smythe's granddaughter had packed her a bag and was flying off with her. 'Make sure ya pick up those casseroles,' Mrs Smythe ordered after she was settled in the helicopter.

'I will,' Halley assured her, and with that she walked back towards Max, neither of them moving until the helicopter was up and away. She pulled her coat closer around her. All she wanted was for Max to take her in his arms, tell her that he loved her, beg her to move here permanently to be his new partner and then propose to her.

'You'd better get those casseroles,' he murmured, before walking away.

Halley grimaced and closed her eyes momentarily. 'Close, but no cigar!'

She said goodnight to the nursing staff and headed back to her car. At Mrs Smythe's house, she found her granddaughter's husband who had placed the casseroles into the box and helped Halley carry them to her car.

When she arrived home, she left two of the large casserole dishes in the box by Max's front door and carried the remaining one into her house. After heating it up she spooned some food onto a plate and forced herself to eat. It was delicious as usual but she just couldn't work up an appetite. She felt miserable.

During the past week and a half she'd become so involved in this community and felt as though she was betraying them with her evaluation. Next time, she told herself as she did the dishes, keep your distance.

She settled down with her paperwork to try and figure out if she'd missed anything, *any* error that might force the situation in the other direction. She heard Max come home and listened intently to the muted sounds of him moving about his house. Soon everything became quiet and she returned her attention back to her work. It didn't happen.

Her eyes misted over with tears at the thought of leaving. She'd let Max down, she'd let the community down, and by becoming so involved she'd let herself down. More than anything, Halley desperately wanted to stay. She would love to work alongside Max every day. To share his thoughts, his smiles, his kisses!

She sniffed and wiped the tears away. It wasn't to be. Max was going to marry Christina and that was all there was to it. No way could she stay, seeing him every day, knowing he wouldn't be coming home with her every night.

She packed up her work and buried her head in the pillow, crying herself to sleep over her hopeless situation.

CHAPTER ELEVEN

THE next two days were very painful for Halley. Seeing Max, working with Max and loving him so completely almost made it hard for her to breathe.

By Friday afternoon she was mentally exhausted from holding on to her emotions when saying goodbye to her patients. Clarabelle had been the worst, but the two women had promised to keep in touch.

'You're letting him get away,' Clarabelle had insisted just before Halley had left.

'He was never mine to have in the first place,' she'd clarified unhappily.

All that was left to do now was to hand over to Max. She did this at the hospital, also ensuring that she'd signed off on each patient's set of case-notes.

'I think that's it,' she said finally and looked across at him.

'Good.' Max gave her a brisk nod and returned his attention to the paperwork he'd been completing when she'd walked in.

When he didn't say anything else, she stood. 'Well, then, I guess I'll go and clean out my desk.'

'Hmm?' he asked vaguely, glancing up at her.

'Nothing,' she said, and walked quickly from his office. She managed to control the tears while she gathered her files and bag, although the lump in her throat refused to move. 'I guess that's it,' she said, looking around the office once more.

She hesitated momentarily, her gaze drifting in the direction of Max's office, but she quickly continued on her way, out of the front doors and to her car. Ridiculous, she thought as she drove back to the duplex.

When she arrived, it was to find some of the women waiting for her.

'Hi,' Christina said brightly. Alice was there from the bakery, and Kylie, the district nurse, so was Sheena and a few of the nursing staff.

'What's going on?' Halley asked.

'Girls' night out,' Christina announced with a laugh. 'Come on. We have dinner reservations at the Chinese restaurant.'

Halley smiled, deeply touched at the thought. She allowed herself to be bundled into someone's car, and as they walked into the restaurant a little later, Halley whispered to Christina, 'Did you mastermind this?'

'Yes,' Christina replied proudly.

'Good for you.' Halley nodded. Whether the change in Christina had anything to do with Jon or not, Halley was impressed with how the young woman had become more independent.

'I've been spending a lot of time with Gran this week,' Christina admitted.

'So she said.'

'And it's made me realise that…I can do whatever I want to do.' Christina's eyes were wide with wonder.

'Yes.'

Christina frowned slightly. 'Now all I need to figure out is *what* I want.'

Halley laughed. 'That's always the trickiest bit.'

The waiter came to take their order and the night progressed with a mass of giggles and girl-talk, all of which Halley knew she'd miss terribly when she left the next morning.

'You could always stay,' Sheena ventured, and the other women agreed.

Halley avoided looking at Christina. 'It's a nice thought and, believe it or not, you're not the first one to suggest it, but it just wouldn't work out.'

'Why not?' Christina asked, and Halley felt her heart pound faster at the thought of telling this nice woman that she was in love with her fiancé.

'Well... Because...' she fumbled, trying to think of the right thing to say.

'I mean, you and Max seem to work well together,' Christina added. 'And the living arrangements are already organised.'

'You know the patients,' Sheena added.

Halley looked at all the smiling faces before her and almost broke down in tears. Instead she straightened her shoulders and forced a smile. 'I have to report back to the VDH first, and no doubt they have somewhere else they need me to go.' She'd hoped there was a hint of finality in her tone and as their fried ice cream arrived at the moment, she was spared any more questions.

When she was finally taken home, Halley felt more miserable than before. Why did she have to like the people so much? Why did they have to like her back? Why did she have to be in love with a man she couldn't have?

Slowly and methodically, she packed up her belongings. She wanted to be ready to leave as soon as she woke next morning. If she hadn't been feeling so washed out and fatigued she'd have left right there and then, but she'd only be risking an accident if she did.

Once again, Halley cried herself to sleep. Never had she been so miserable in all her life.

Max woke with a start. What was that noise? He glanced at the clock—it was just before six. The noise came again.

It was as though someone was moving furniture. His sluggish brain came to life as he realised that Halley was shifting her furniture back.

She was leaving.

He felt an emptiness begin to consume him at the thought of never seeing her again. His heart ached and his head pounded. Max clenched his teeth as he made himself listen to reason.

Halley was all wrong for him. They'd both known it from the start.

So why did everything about her feel so right? When she smiled at him he felt as though the sun would shine for ever. When she laughed a feeling of happiness engulfed him. When she gazed at him with those wide brown eyes filled with desire he wanted nothing more than to scoop her up and kiss her senseless.

Max groaned and buried his head beneath the pillow. She'd told him that if he found another permanent GP the hospital would remain open. All he had to do was get up, go next door and beg her to stay… But if he did that he'd be forced to see her, work with her every single day.

The past two weeks had been bad enough! The woman drove him insane. He couldn't think properly, his routine was out of whack and his libido was definitely out of control. He was all about neatness and order. Everything had a place—except Halley Ryan. She had no place in his life, he reminded himself sternly.

If he gave in to his emotions, she would love him and eventually leave him. He'd be no better off than his father. He would turn into a grumpy, irritable old man, doomed to face the rest of his life alone.

The furniture stopped moving and moments later he heard the heavy thud of her front door closing. He stayed still, listening as she revved the Jaguar to life on the cold wintry morning. Soon she was pulling out onto the road and the sound of the engine died away in the distance. She was gone.

Max forced himself to breathe again. Hopefully now he could get his life back on track.

On Monday night, after he and Christina had finished eating dinner, Max noticed his fiancée fidgeting with her pearls again. She'd done it a few times during dinner when there'd been a lull in the conversation.

'Leave the coffee,' he said to Christina. 'Come and sit down.'

'It's no trouble, Max,' she replied.

Max stood and walked over to her. He took both of her hands in his and led her over to a chair. 'Please, Christina. We need to talk.'

Her hand went immediately to the pearls and he wondered exactly what it was that was making her nervous. Was it him or something else? Or should he say…*someone* else? He opened his mouth to speak.

'Max—I can't.' She stood again and took a step away from him.

'Can't what?' he asked gently after a moment's silence.

'I…I can't marry you,' she blurted, and then sighed with relief. She gazed at him earnestly. 'I've been trying to tell you for about a week now but just didn't know how to say it.'

'Is it Jon?'

A smile spread across Christina's face and she nodded, her hand dropping from her pearls. 'Yes. I love him, Max.' The words were said with awe and wonderment. 'He's coming back to town in a few days so I knew I had to tell you before then.'

Max stood and crossed to her side, a warm smile lighting his face. 'I'm very happy for you, Christina.'

'You're not angry?' Her eyes were wide with astonishment.

'No. I'm very happy for you.'

Halley delivered her recommendation to the Victorian Department for Health and was pleased to discover they were going to follow it. She kept praying that Max would find someone so the hospital could remain open. She'd felt compelled to make some enquiries herself, but so far had come up empty.

Nine days after leaving Heartfield, she was feeling horrible. She could feel the beginnings of a cold coming on, and as she was hardly sleeping or eating the cold would no doubt take hold. Right at the moment, she didn't have the energy to care.

Halley had received a call from her colleague, Brian Newton, at Melbourne Hospital, informing her that a Mr Alan Kempsey was an inpatient and was asking to see her.

Surprised, Halley went to the hospital. 'Alan,' she said with a smile as she walked into his room. 'Nice to see you again.'

'Likewise.' Alan gave her a close scrutiny. 'You're not looking too good, Halley. Been burning the midnight oil?'

'Something like that,' she answered vaguely. 'So, Brian, your surgeon, told me that you were back to check your fracture and they found it wasn't healing properly.'

'Yeah. So now I'm stuck in here for a few days.'

'Did Agnes travel with you?'

'No. She doesn't like big cities. I'm a big boy now,' he said. 'I don't need my sister to hold my hand all the time.'

Halley laughed. 'So…any news from Heartfield?' She

desperately wanted to hear about Max but there was no way she was going to ask.

'I thought Jupiter would have told you what was happening. He's been there enough in the past week or so.'

'I haven't had a chance to catch up with him.'

'He's a great guy. He's dropped around to my place a few times and we've talked climbing, which has been really great.' Alan's eyes sparkled with a bit of hero-worship. 'Imagine that. A legend like Jupiter in *my* home!'

'Imagine,' she echoed.

He told her about Dan's excitement at the new Planet Electronics plant and how Jupiter had been staying at Dan's home.

'Really?'

No wonder Jon hadn't been returning her calls. She wondered what Max thought about it.

They chatted for a while longer before Alan reached out to take Halley's hand in his. 'It's *really* good to see you, Halley,' he said, his eyes shining with admiration. The way he held her hand caused a prickle of apprehension to wash over her. His fingers were soft and sensual around her own, his index finger moving back and forth, gently caressing. Slowly Halley extracted her hand from his.

'Listen, Alan, I—'

'It's Max, isn't it?'

'Pardon?'

'Max. You're in love with him, aren't you?'

Halley sighed. What now? She looked down at the ground for a moment before returning her gaze to meet his. Despite what he felt for her, she owed Alan the truth. 'Yes.'

Alan closed his eyes in pain and nodded. 'I thought as much.' He looked at her again and forced a smile. 'Can't blame a guy for trying.' He shrugged.

'Alan, it's just that—'

'Friends?' he asked, and she nodded.

'I'd like that.'

She stayed for another ten minutes as they continued talking about rock-climbing. She left with the excuse that she had a lunch date with Marty and went to the head office of Planet Electronics. She was greeted warmly by the staff, and when Marty's secretary informed her that he was still in a meeting Halley waited in his office.

'Hey, Squirt,' Marty said a few minutes later when he walked in. Halley was sitting at his desk, sharpening all his pencils and tidying the messy pile of papers. 'Sorry. Meeting ran overtime. Ready to eat?'

'Ah…sure. Give me a second.' She reorganised his top stationery drawer, ensuring all of the self-adhesive notes were arranged in size order.

'What's with you?' Marty asked.

'What?' Halley looked at him blankly.

'Halley, you're tidying my desk! You're the queen of chaos. So give… What's with you?'

Halley sighed and finished making sure his desk blotter was perfectly straight. 'I don't know, Marty. I guess I'm feeling a little…'

'Lonely?' He supplied. 'Missing Max more than you thought you would? Unable to pull your life together?'

Halley laughed ironically but it ended on a choked sob. 'Am I *that* obvious?'

Marty gave her a hug. 'You never know what might happen.'

'Anyway,' she said as she stood and prowled around his room, 'are we going to lunch or not?'

Marty's phone shrilled to life and he quickly picked it up. 'Martin Ryan.' Halley watched him as he listened to whoever was on the other end of the phone. 'We're going to the Cottage for lunch. Now. All right, we'll meet you there.'

'Who was that?' Halley asked.

'Jon.'

'Back in town, is he?'

'Obviously,' her brother teased, and laughed. 'Come on, Squirt. Let's go.'

Halley brightened up in her brother's company, and she was looking forward to seeing Jon and grilling him about life in Heartfield. They had just been seated when she saw her brother, towering over everyone else, heading in their direction.

Seconds later her mouth was hanging open in disbelief at the person who was standing next to him—holding his hand!

'*Christina!*' Halley shot to her feet.

'Oh, Halley,' the other woman bubbled, and let go of Jon's hand long enough to wrap her arms around Halley. 'Isn't it wonderful?'

Halley was completely speechless. *Never* had she seen Christina so…effervescent. She looked at Jon, who was smiling as well.

'We've shocked her, Chrissy,' he said, and Halley slumped back down into the chair.

'Wh-what—? How—?'

Christina and Jon sat down, pulling their chairs close together. 'We're in love,' Jon told her.

'I did it, Halley. I stood up to my father and said I wasn't going to marry Max and that I loved Jon.'

'A-and what did Dan say?'

Jon grinned. 'He couldn't have been happier.'

Halley's eyes felt as though they were about to pop out. 'What about *Max*?'

'I don't love Max,' Christina stated as she gazed at Jon. 'Not in the way I love *Jon*.'

'There you go, Halley,' Marty said. 'He's free. Go get him.'

'*Martin!*' Halley turned her horrified gaze from her brother to Christina.

'You love Max?'

Halley couldn't take it any longer. She crumpled into a heap at the table and buried her head in her hands. Her emotions had been so taut, so highly strung for what seemed an eternity, and now it turned out that Max was free! He was available! He was there for her to love without guilt!

'Is *that* the reason why you didn't want to stay in Heartfield?' Christina asked, and Halley raised her head to look at her. She looked radiant. Happy. And the pearls were gone. That said more than anything to Halley. Christina was a woman who had found herself. Who had taken a huge step and reached out for happiness. Was it possible Halley could do the same?

'Ah…something like that.'

'Can we get this lunch over and done with?' Jon said impatiently.

'We're going engagement-ring shopping afterwards,' Christina told her excitedly.

'But you hardly know each other,' Halley said.

'So? You hardly know Max,' Jon retorted. 'When you know, you just…*know*.'

'I knew the night of the Christmas dinner.' Christina gazed up at the man of her dreams. 'All I had to do then was to get up the nerve to take control of my life.' She turned to Halley. 'If it hadn't been for you and Gran urging me to do what I needed to do, then I doubt I'd be sitting here today.'

'Come on,' Jon said again. 'Let's eat. We have some important shopping to do.'

Halley found it hard to concentrate on anything other than the fact that Max was free! What should she do now? Should she apply for the job at Heartfield District Hospital? Should she wait for him to make the first move?

They'd admitted an attraction to each other but she knew that Max still had other reservations about her. Besides, attraction didn't equal love.

Her heart and mind were in an even bigger turmoil after they left the restaurant.

For the next two days Halley was as nervous as a long-tailed cat in a room full of rocking chairs. Every time her phone rang she hoped it would be Max. Every time someone knocked on her door she prayed it would be him.

Nothing! Not a word.

Dejection started to set in on the third day as her hope started to take a dive. She needed to think. She needed to get away and think. The VDH had offered her another assignment on the other side of Victoria, and she was deliberating over whether or not to accept. She asked for a further forty-eight hours to think it over.

Halley called her parents, who lived in the Victorian snowfields, asking if she could come stay for a few days.

'We're heading to Melbourne in a few hours,' her mother said. 'Jon wants us to meet our future daughter-in-law.'

'You'll love her, Mum, but if you don't mind I think I'll pass on the family reunion. I need some time away from everything.'

'No word from Max?' her mother asked, the concern evident in her voice.

'No,' Halley said, trying not to choke on the word.

'I'll get everything ready for you here,' her mother said.

'If you leave now, you'll get here before we go. You've got plenty of clothes already here, so hang up the phone and get in the car,' she urged.

'Good idea,' Halley replied, and followed her mother's advice.

The drive was soothing to Halley's frazzled nerves, and when she arrived her parents both embraced her before setting off on their own journey.

Halley prowled around the house, tidying things and reorganising the clothes she kept at her parents' house. She peered through her father's telescope but didn't find any solace in the stars. She changed into a pair of her favourite boxer shorts and old top she used to sleep in. Next she removed her contacts and slipped on her glasses. She was just far too exhausted to be bothered with her contacts at the moment. The house was warm from the fire her father had lit in the slow combustion stove that morning. Taking a litre of double chocolate chip ice cream out of the freezer, she rugged up in a blanket and sat down to watch a movie on television.

She was starting to feel a bit better. Comfortable clothes, comfort food, a good movie to watch and the security of her parents' home. So what if Max didn't want her? She'd get by. She always had before.

Just before the end of the movie, she thought she heard a car engine outside the house. She switched the television off so she could hear better before tiptoeing over to the door and peering out into the dark night. She couldn't see anything but the noise had stopped. She shrugged and headed back to the lounge.

Firm knocking on the door startled her, and she screamed.

'Halley?'

It was *Max*!

'Halley? Are you all right? Open up.' He knocked even harder.

She forced her legs to work and almost flew to the door, which she wrenched open to find him standing on the other side. A blast of cold air swirled into the house, making her shiver.

Neither of them moved. They were both caught in the moment—the moment of seeing each other again. Questions, such as what he was doing there, seemed irrelevant. He *was* here and that was all that mattered. He looked incredible in his navy business suit and her heart rate increased even more.

Halley shivered again and Max groaned as he took in the sight of her. As though he could control himself no longer, he took two steps forward, gathered her firmly into his arms, kicked the door shut with his foot and pressed his lips to hers.

Halley melted against him, wondering momentarily if she was dreaming once more. It felt better than a dream. *He* felt better than a dream. He lifted her up into his arms and carried her to the lounge, his lips never once leaving hers.

Max sat down with Halley on his lap as his mouth plundered her own, unable to believe that he was finally kissing her.

Every nerve-ending in her body was alive with delight, devotion and desire. She pulled her mouth away momentarily and gazed into his blue eyes. 'Oh, Max. I love you,' she whispered.

His answer was to claim her lips once more, the sensations so mind-numbing, so fulfilling, so perfect. Finally he pulled back. Their breathing was ragged and uneven. 'I've been wanting to kiss you for so long, Halley,' he groaned, as he nuzzled her neck.

Halley closed her eyes, unable to believe this was really happening. Max's hand slid down her legs. He raised his head and she opened her eyes. 'Legs!' A slow, sexy smile spread across his face. 'You *really* do have them,' he jested and she smiled back, happiness bursting forth within her.

'I love you,' she said again, and sighed, feeling comfortable and content in his arms.

'So you've said.' Max smiled and kissed her again. 'You were right, Halley.'

'About what?'

'About marriage. It *is* about commitment and support. It *is* about sharing and loving. It *is* about finding your soulmate and spending the rest of your life with them. It just took me longer to realise that *you* were *my* soul-mate.'

'Oh, Max,' Halley breathed, deeply touched by his words. Her eyes misted with tears, but for the first time in weeks they were tears of happiness. He tenderly removed her glasses and placed them on the coffee table.

'When Christina and I ended our engagement, I felt nothing but relief. My feelings for you were so prominent, so passionate that I was terrified to trust them.' Max raked a hand through his hair and smiled down at her. 'I didn't know how you would react to me turning up on your doorstep. You said you were attracted to me but whether it went further than that I wasn't sure.

'Then, to top everything off, I was called to Geelong to discuss the possibility of the hospital entering into a co-operative agreement with one of the specialist centres.'

'What was the outcome?' Halley asked anxiously. She felt responsible for the hospital's fate but didn't want Max to be here just because he wanted her as the second GP.

'It's all signed, sealed and delivered. Heartfield District Hospital won't be closing its doors anytime soon. There is, however, room for one more GP—if you're interested, of course.'

'Do you think I'd really be able to pass up an opportunity of being with you every day? Working with you.' Her eyes glazed over with passion. 'Living with you.'

Max groaned and pressed his lips to hers. 'The entire time I was in negotiations, all I could think about was finding you and telling you how I felt,' he said softly against her mouth.

'And how is that?' Halley held her breath, waiting for his answer.

'I love you, Halley.'

Halley giggled, giddy with delight.

'I've been terrified of ending up like my father. He loved my mother and she left him.'

'I know,' she soothed, and kissed him.

'I thought if I didn't allow myself to love as passionately as he had, then I'd be fine. Then *you* came along.'

'And blew all your neat and orderly plans out of the water.'

Max nodded. 'Yes… And I can't thank you enough.' His gaze darkened and his voice was husky when he murmured, 'I ache for you, Halley. I need you so much that I can't think straight.' Max pressed his lips to hers and once more Halley was blown away by the fact that she was now allowed to kiss him—whenever she wanted.

When he pulled back, he kissed her nose and lifted her from his lap. 'Wait here,' he instructed.

'Where…?' she protested, but he was already out of the door. She heard a car door open and then close before his footsteps headed back. He closed the door behind him, a large square box in his hands.

He placed the box on the coffee-table and took two cake forks out of his jacket pocket. 'Open the box.'

Halley did as he suggested, amazed to notice that her hands were trembling slightly. She raised the lid. It was a chocolate mud cake and piped onto the top were the words, MARRY ME.

'Well?' he asked, and she was surprised at the uncertainty in his tone.

'Yes. Yes, Max.' Halley laughed and pressed her lips to his. 'Yes.'

Max scooped up a piece of cake and held his fork in front of Halley's mouth. 'Let's seal the deal by devouring this delicious cake.'

'Brilliant idea.'

She made them coffee and they snuggled on the lounge, talking softly and making plans for their life together. 'I was going to buy you a ring but I have no idea what you like.' He shook his head. 'There's still so much about you that I don't know.'

'But we have the rest of our lives to find out,' she replied happily.

Max pulled back slightly and looked down into her eyes. 'Would you *really* wear white leather to our wedding?'

Halley smiled impishly at him and wiggled her eyebrows. 'Of course.'

Max groaned in delight. 'You in white leather. At least I won't have to worry about coveting your perfect legs in public.'

'What do you mean? I'm talking about a white leather *mini*-skirt.'

He closed his eyes and nuzzled her neck. 'Don't torture me.'

'Why not?' she replied softly. 'It's my job!'

Modern Romance™
...seduction and
passion guaranteed

Tender Romance™
...love affairs that
last a lifetime

Sensual Romance™
...sassy, sexy and
seductive

Blaze™
...sultry days and
steamy nights

Medical Romance™
...medical drama on
the pulse

Historical Romance™
...rich, vivid and
passionate

27 new titles every month.

*With all kinds of Romance for
every kind of mood...*

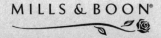

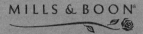

FREE

2 BOOKS
AND A SURPRISE GIFT!

We would like to take this opportunity to thank you for reading this Mills & Boon® book by offering you the chance to take TWO more specially selected titles from the Medical Romance™ series absolutely FREE! We're also making this offer to introduce you to the benefits of the Reader Service™—

- ★ FREE home delivery
- ★ FREE monthly Newsletter
- ★ FREE gifts and competitions
- ★ Exclusive Reader Service discount
- ★ Books available before they're in the shops

Accepting these FREE books and gift places you under no obligation to buy; you may cancel at any time, even after receiving your free shipment. Simply complete your details below and return the entire page to the address below. *You don't even need a stamp!*

YES! Please send me 2 free Medical Romance books and a surprise gift. I understand that unless you hear from me, I will receive 4 superb new titles every month for just £2.55 each, postage and packing free. I am under no obligation to purchase any books and may cancel my subscription at any time. The free books and gift will be mine to keep in any case.

M2ZEC

Ms/Mrs/Miss/Mr ....Initials ....
BLOCK CAPITALS PLEASE

Surname ....

Address ....

....

....Postcode ....

Send this whole page to:
UK: FREEPOST CN81, Croydon, CR9 3WZ
EIRE: PO Box 4546, Kilcock, County Kildare (stamp required)

Offer valid in UK and Eire only and not available to current Reader Service subscribers to this series. We reserve the right to refuse an application and applicants must be aged 18 years or over. Only one application per household. Terms and prices subject to change without notice. Offer expires 30th September 2002. As a result of this application, you may receive offers from other carefully selected companies. If you would prefer not to share in this opportunity please write to The Data Manager at the address above.

Mills & Boon® is a registered trademark owned by Harlequin Mills & Boon Limited.
Medical Romance™ is being used as a trademark.